SO-CFR-500

Alex tapped the camera placed next to her door. "Doesn't a camera light usually come on? A red light?"

She grabbed her phone. No notifications. Alex was right. Her phone should be chirping with their movements. Teddy's spine stiffened like it did when he caught a scent. He spun around in a circle, lifting his nose up and down rapidly. He touched his nose to the door, barked and then looked pointedly at Violet.

Alex flinched. "His bark sounds like a gunshot. Tired of being in the cold, huh, buddy?"

"Be glad he doesn't bark often." She tried to keep her voice light, but it trembled. Teddy's golden eyes told her everything she needed to know. She stepped to the side of the door so the window insert wouldn't reveal her location if anyone was still inside. She beckoned Alex. "Do you want to call the police, or is it still best to keep this to ourselves?"

"What is it? What did you see?"

"Teddy's reaction. He's found a scent that doesn't belong here. I think someone might be inside."

Heather Woodhaven earned her pilot's license, rode a hot-air balloon over the safari lands of Kenya, parasailed over Caribbean seas, lived through an accidental detour onto a black-diamond ski trail in Aspen, and snorkeled among stingrays before becoming a mother of three and wife of one. She channels her love for adventure into writing characters who find themselves in extraordinary circumstances.

Books by Heather Woodhaven

Love Inspired Suspense

Texas Takedown
Tracking Secrets
Credible Threat
Protected Secrets
Wilderness Sabotage
Deadly River Pursuit
Search and Defend

Alaska K-9 Unit

Arctic Witness

True Blue K-9 Unit: Brooklyn

Chasing Secrets

Twins Separated at Birth

Undercover Twin
Covert Christmas Twin

Visit the Author Profile page at LoveInspired.com.

SEARCH AND DEFEND

HEATHER WOODHAVEN

LOVE INSPIRED SUSPENSE
INSPIRATIONAL ROMANCE

LOVE INSPIRED® SUSPENSE
INSPIRATIONAL ROMANCE

ISBN-13: 978-1-335-73596-6

Search and Defend

Copyright © 2021 by Heather Humrichouse

For questions and comments about the quality of this book, please contact us at CustomerService@Harlequin.com.

Love Inspired
22 Adelaide St. West, 40th Floor
Toronto, Ontario M5H 4E3, Canada
www.LoveInspired.com

Printed in U.S.A.

My flesh and my heart faileth: but God is the strength
of my heart, and my portion for ever.
—*Psalms* 73:26

To all my family and friends. Your unique variety of expertise and knowledge has been a great benefit to me. Thank you for responding to my out-of-the-blue texts filled with questions and what-ifs.

ONE

FBI special agent Alex Driscoll hated undercover work. Pretending to be someone else tied his gut up in knots, especially when he no longer had a partner to watch his back. Tonight, he was playing the part of a chef. His informant had told him to watch for the handoff of a flash drive to a woman with jet-black hair and a red dress. The private political fundraiser was being held the night after Christmas, though, which meant he'd already spotted thirteen women who matched that description.

"My table wants ours made special order. No ginger, no celery, extra avocado with a light drizzle of wasabi." The woman in front of him raised a heavily jeweled hand. "Too much, and I'll send it back. The rice on the outside, not the inside." She demanded perfection, as did most of the attendees, given they'd all paid two thousand dollars to attend the special event.

"Of course, ma'am." The position with the catering company should've been the perfect cover since he enjoyed cooking, but he wasn't sure he could deliver under the scrutiny of the rich and famous. Sushi was an especially difficult dish to make while keeping watch on the guests. "What led you to attend tonight, ma'am?" he asked as an excuse to look up and scan the room.

Cooking stations lined the back side of the lodge located at the base of the mountain. The building was set apart from the rest of the famous Idaho ski resort. The glass walls on the opposite side of where he stood offered dazzling views of the lit-up ski runs that were closed during the event.

"We support Governor Davenport wholeheartedly." She cocked an eyebrow. "Why else would anyone be here?"

"It's the event of the season." He flashed what he hoped would be his most charming smile. All Alex knew was there was going to be an assassination attempt in the next couple of weeks. The target would be someone powerful, not necessarily the governor. The flash drive Alex hoped to intercept was rumored to contain the name of the target and their itinerary. One of the many women wearing a red dress would be the Firecracker's courier.

He added a dash of black sesame seeds to the top of the roll and handed the sushi plate to the waiter standing by. "What table, ma'am?"

"Seven." She strode off, chin held high, and the waiter hustled after her.

If the Firecracker intended on taking out the governor, he might also be here tonight, discreetly gathering intel on his prey. The same intel Alex needed in order to stop him once and for all.

The assassin's modus operandi usually involved killing the target along with their security detail. Bombs were his choice of weapon. The Firecracker had never targeted a large amount of people at once, like the couple of hundred in attendance now, but Alex wasn't lowering his guard. Every chance he got to slip away, he searched for nooks and crannies in the lodge where explosives might be hidden.

The FBI had no descriptions to go on, no photographs, only that the assassin was in his late fifties. Unfortunately, that meant Alex was surrounded by potential suspects mingling within the party. The lodge was one giant room with floor-to-ceiling windows facing one of the resort's mountains. The other three walls were decorated to resemble a log cabin, a luxury, multimillion dollar one.

At his two o'clock, a man with eyes darting left and right hastily made his way across the room. Under five foot ten, the man was average in height and looks, early thirties. He would've blended in if his right hand hadn't been clenched in a tight fist. Either the man planned to punch someone, or he was carrying the flash drive.

"I heard we talk to you if we want a special order." An elderly woman stepped in front of his station, blocking his view.

Alex looked over her shoulder. "Yes. Shortly. I believe we're out of…" He lost his train of thought as his gaze tracked the man's path. A glittering party clutch sat upright at one of the tables, open and waiting. Six feet away from the table, a woman in red laughed loudly at something another woman said.

"We're out of some ingredients. I'll go and get them from another station. Please check back in a few minutes." He stepped out from behind the station and barely registered the irritated huff. "Pardon me." He jostled in and out of groups in his way, fighting to keep his eye on the one-fisted man.

"Do you need something?" A waiter blocked his path. "You left your station."

"Yes, I need to grab something from another chef. I'll be right back."

Like running through a complicated football play, Alex spun right and darted left to avoid colliding with other guests. There. The man's fist released right over the top of the clutch. The slightest reflection of silver confirmed his suspicions. Alex reached into his white chef's jacket and grabbed the flash drive he'd prepared. Except the woman in red was starting to turn around, no doubt to retrieve the clutch now that the handoff had been made.

Alex had to stall her. He slipped his left foot out, and a man tripped over him, diving headfirst into a group of four. The exclamations drew attention, and just as he'd hoped, the woman in red watched, her brow furrowed. Alex darted behind her, made a one-handed switch and continued to the chef station closest to her table. "I need…salt at my station," he said.

"Then get it from the kitchen. I need mine." The chef scowled before beaming at an approaching guest.

Alex didn't mind at all. Mission accomplished. The woman turned back to her purse, and seeing the flash drive Alex had placed there, closed the clutch and smiled. She hadn't noticed him make the switch. Good. Tonight, they would finally bring the Firecracker to justice.

There were two men staring right at him from across the room. They had broad shoulders under their tuxedos and matching gaits as they started toward him. Alex didn't think they were the Idaho state troopers that were typically assigned to the governor. The telltale wrinkle in their jackets gave him pause. Armed. Unfortunately, Alex had been searched "for security reasons" before being allowed to enter as a chef. His own gun was still in the car.

He darted toward the north wall, making his way around the attendees to get back to his station. A quick look over his shoulder confirmed the men were coming for him. He needed to get the flash drive somewhere safe in case they were associates of the Firecracker.

A woman with caramel hair down to her shoulders, dressed in a shimmering silver gown and strappy heels he'd never imagined she'd be caught dead in stepped into the light.

Violet Sharp, his partner's widow.

Rick Sharp had been killed by the Firecracker two years ago. Violet's face blanched at the sight of him, but she didn't raise a hand or an arm in greeting. Thankfully, she knew better.

Violet had never been the type to attend ritzy political fundraisers, but grief changed people. He'd also never seen her without her K-9 Search and Rescue dog by her side. She blinked rapidly and broke the unspoken connection, turning away to offer a tight smile to a tall, athletic-looking man who embraced her and gave her a little-too-friendly kiss to the cheek.

Alex had hesitated too long. The two men had almost reached him. He continued his path toward Violet and bumped into her shoulder.

"Hey, watch where you're going," the man with her said.

Alex grabbed Violet's elbow as if offering support, all the while dropping the drive into the main compartment of the silver purse hanging at her side. "Terribly sorry, ma'am."

Her eyes widened. "No harm done."

He strode past her, jostling and bumping past other people lest the two men suspect and target Violet. The crowd was getting irritated with him. All the more reason to feign excuses and leave early.

He sidestepped left and reached his food station just as they did.

"Enjoying the party?" the one to the left asked.

"Isn't that what people do?" He shrugged. "I'm not feeling well, though. So I think I'll be leaving early."

"How about we escort you outside then?"

He'd walked straight into that one. "It's cold out there. Looks like snow falling again. How about I—?"

The man to his right flashed open his jacket to reveal a gun with a silencer attached. "Let's go. You wouldn't want anyone else to get hurt, would you?"

Were they referring to someone specific or bluffing? Alex narrowed his eyes. "What you're suggesting would draw a lot of attention. I—"

He'd been focused on the man with the gun instead of the one on the left. His second mistake of the night. A needle pricked through his white jacket and into his arm. He reached out and grabbed the man's hand and yanked the needle back out. The syringe hit the floor, and Alex stomped on it, crushing the vial.

The telltale sensation of heat in his veins and a racing heart rate meant he hadn't pulled out the needle fast enough. He could call out, make a scene, but that might put Violet in danger. As a law enforcement ranger for the US Forest Service, she'd run to his aid. He'd never forgive himself if his decision resulted in her losing her life, too.

"What'd you give me?" he asked. The governor had yet to arrive. The two men were both too young to match the Firecracker's description.

"You're about to find out."

Alex moved to grab the knife on the cart in front of him, but his hand missed the handle and pushed the bowl of chopped green onions instead.

"What did you…?" His voice slurred. His vision blurred. The two men hooked their elbows through his, and he lost his footing. A moment later, cold air stung his face. But his eyes wouldn't stay open long enough to find out where he was going, and he didn't think he'd live long enough to find out.

Violet Sharp could not believe Alex was here. She knew enough of her late husband's work to never wave at another special agent. Ever. If an agent greeted her or waved first, then it was safe. Alex had seen her—bumped into her, even—but he hadn't acknowledged her in a personal way. Her eyes had wanted to follow him when he'd moved past her, but she hadn't wanted to draw any attention to him.

Dark wavy hair, green eyes and only a few inches taller than her, he appeared intimidating in size because of his athletic build. He looked different than the last time she'd seen him, like he was made of harder edges.

In the one second their eyes had connected, she'd recognized the pain he carried, certain she reflected the same hollow emptiness. Judging by the tension in his jaw, he had felt the same way about seeing her. They reminded each other of the greatest loss in their lives. Rick. The sensation had rocked her off balance. After two years, she shouldn't be so caught off guard by sudden waves of sorrow, but grief refused to follow any rule book.

She also really needed a word with her best friend. Eryn Lane had pleaded with her to come to this party. The only reason Violet had agreed was so that Eryn could have a night out without kids. She'd foolishly assumed the evening would be free of any of the matchmaking attempts her friends had been intent on lately. Eryn had ambushed her by arranging for Violet's high school boyfriend, Bruce Wilkinson, to meet them there.

Every social invitation had become a minefield the past couple of months. It was as if crossing the two-year marker of being a widow had put an Available sign on her forehead. Why couldn't Eryn get it through her head that Violet had no intention of marrying again?

Bruce was regaling them with yet another story of one of his latest business ventures when a current of cold air rushed past her.

"Who keeps opening the door?" Eryn wrapped her arms around herself and turned to find the source of the cold. Two men, one on either side of Alex, disappeared out the back.

"Looks like someone had a little too much Christmas cheer," Bruce muttered. "That guy was bumping into everyone, not just you. And he's one of the employees, no less. If this were my business, I would—"

Violet didn't hear the rest of Bruce's analysis on best business practices. The back of her neck tingled. Something wasn't right. There was nothing behind the lodge but woods. The same woods she'd planned to walk through to get home. "Excuse me, I need to check on Teddy."

She grabbed a napkin from Alex's food station on her way to the coatrack and threw on her wool coat and the boots she'd brought with her. A moment later, she was out the front door next to the parking lot.

Teddy, her Newfoundland dog, sat at attention beside the valet, Daniella Curtis. The sidewalk in front of the lodge had been converted to a red-carpet platform. Daniella managed a podium with little hooks to keep track of vehicle keys.

"Thanks for letting Teddy keep you company." Where Violet went, Teddy went. The town understood that her K-9 never left her side. Leaving him with Daniella had been a compromise after Eryn had expressed her displeasure at bringing the dog along. Even when Violet wasn't on duty with the USFS, she was always on duty for search and rescue. "Has Teddy been a good guest?"

"Of course." Daniella patted the top of the massive dog's head. "He's keeping me from being bored out of my mind."

When Teddy sat upright, he measured over two feet from shoulder to ground. From nose to tail, he was six feet long and weighed thirty pounds more than Violet, though she wasn't about to reveal that specific amount to anyone. Her gentle giant was the best search-and-rescue dog in the area and a loyal companion.

She patted her side. "Teddy and I need to check on something. We should be right back." She set the strappy heels and sparkly purse behind Daniella's podium. She didn't need anything flapping on her person, hindering her speed. "Mind if I leave these here?"

Violet didn't wait for Daniella's answer. She ran around the corner of the lodge. Teddy didn't need prodding. He ran at her side. Plenty of breeds had the sniffing capabilities to work in search and rescue, but Teddy had the type of intelligence that was rare. The back of the building was deserted, but two sets of footprints in the snow led to the woods.

The breeze had faded, and the winter night seemed to be holding its breath. Her time working as Teddy's handler had taught her to pay attention to things she'd never noticed before. She could hear her own heart beating. There was no sign of anyone else rushing after Alex. She had to know if he was okay, Rick would want her to make sure. If Alex didn't want her there, she'd simply pretend she was out walking her dog.

She presented the napkin she'd snagged from Alex's food station. Teddy lifted his nose and made staccato-like inhalations.

"Find."

A whisper was all he needed. His head disappeared into the powdered snow for a split second before popping back up. His golden eyes and brown bushy fur made him appear like a bear, the inspiration for his name, especially in the snow. And right now, he was the happiest bear in the world. He had caught the scent, and he was eager to go to work.

She rushed after him and entered the woods, where all hint of light from the moon and the stars disappeared. Popping, cracking sounds toyed with her sense of direction. The noise could be footsteps, or it could be sap freezing inside the trees. At only ten degrees, the cold quickly seeped through her long wool coat. Teddy pressed ahead, directing her which way to go.

The powdery snow proved easy to walk across quietly.

"I can't find the flash drive." A male voice reached her ears. "But he's stirring. He got the needle out before the full—"

"Then maybe we make sure he doesn't wake up. Make the call and get our orders."

Violet held out both hands, a signal for Teddy to stop following the trail. She strained to see past the trees. The two men stood with guns drawn over Alex, who lay crumpled in the snow.

A deep, rolling rumble sent shivers up her spine until she realized Teddy was the source. She stepped behind the cover of a thick trunk before the men could see her. She should've realized Teddy knew Alex and could tell he was in danger. A trainer had once told her that people gave off different types of pheromones depending on their intentions. Teddy understood those intentions. If he was worried about what these men wanted with Alex, she was worried.

"What is that?" One of the men looked their way.

The question gave her an idea. Violet made a click with her tongue, and Teddy's gaze shifted to her. She flipped her palm over and raised it to the sky. He lifted up on his hind legs, standing up, a trick they'd been working on for over a year.

"It's either bigfoot or a bear, and I don't want to find out which."

She didn't blame them. Teddy was one of the larger Newfoundland dogs she'd met, and that was saying something. And his growl had the resonance of a wild animal.

"Are you crazy? Put the gun down. We don't have the kind of firepower to take a bear down before he mauls us."

"If he charges, I'm shooting. Bears are beyond my pay grade."

"Leave him. We don't need him anymore anyway. Let's go!"

Violet hastily lowered her hand. Teddy dropped down to his paws but not before he released another guttural growl. The men made quick work of disappearing in the other direction. She counted to ten in case they decided to come back, then she ran for the figure on the ground.

Teddy proved faster and was nuzzling Alex's face when she arrived at his side. Alex had been around often before Rick's death, and he'd always come prepared with treats, ready to win Teddy's affections. Clearly, Teddy remembered.

Alex groaned and reached up, blocking the dog. "No." His voice sounded groggy but clear. She blew out a sigh of relief. Alive. Teddy moved to sniffing the rest of him, no doubt in search of treats.

"It's Violet." She gingerly reached for his wrist lest he attack on instinct. "I won't hurt you. How do you feel?"

He flinched but blinked rapidly. "Violet," he murmured. His heart rate was strong, a little faster than she'd like, but in the normal range. He sat up suddenly. Teddy's tail wagged faster, and he pressed his body into Alex.

"Feel free to hug him to get warm. He holds a lot of heat."

Alex acted as if he was about to take her advice, but instead, he used the quick hug to right himself to standing. He spun around, fully alert. "Where are they?"

"They ran away, leaving you for dead.

They thought this bear might finish you off."

He pointed at Teddy. "Him? You?" He ran a hand over his face and exhaled. "Thank you both."

"Do you know what they gave you?"

"A short dose of something to knock me out. Felt like I was going to sleep for a surgery. I don't think they gave me much. I managed to get the needle out of my arm before he got the plunger down."

"Who were they, Alex?"

He shook his head. "I'm not sure yet. I never meant for you to get involved, though. I hope I didn't put you in danger."

"They said they couldn't find a flash drive on you."

"Violet?" A shrill voice called out from the direction of the party. "Are you in there?"

"Do you have your gun?" Alex reached for her arm, steadying himself.

"No need." She didn't want to explain that she didn't carry one anymore. At least, not right now. "That's my friend checking up on me. I left the party when I saw those men dragging you out. Rumor has it you're an employee who drank too much."

A light flickered through the trees. "Get some help." Bruce's voice rang out loud and clear. "There's a man with his hands on her. I'm coming, Violet!"

"I'm fine," Violet shouted. "Just taking Teddy for a walk. One second."

Alex straightened. "I need to stay undercover."

She pointed in the opposite direction of the men. "I think your cover might already be blown. And what do you want me to tell them?" She thumbed over her shoulder at Bruce and Eryn, still aiming lights in their direction.

"I need to be able to move around the town and resort without everyone knowing I'm an FBI agent."

Her throat tightened. "Is this about

Rick?" His hesitation irritated her. "The Firecracker?"

He flinched. "You know the name? I thought that information was still—"

"Your superiors interviewed me multiple times when Rick was killed." She shrugged, not wanting to relive the days after, the constant questions and analysis of Rick's last words. "I know the Firecracker was responsible, and that he's still out there."

"I think I've almost got him."

"Then I'll help you in whatever way I can." Maybe she would sleep better knowing Rick's killer had finally faced justice. "I grew up here. I know most of the locals. Just tell me what you need. Who should I tell Bruce and Eryn you are?"

"I need a second." He pulled his white jacket off and flipped it inside out, revealing a black jacket. He removed a black tie from inside a pocket and slipped it over his head. The quick change wasn't anything new to her, as she'd seen her husband practice similar moves for undercover missions, but she was still surprised to see the transformation from employee to party attendee. He brushed off the remaining snow from his legs in one motion.

"Lead the way to your friends," he said. "Before we have more company. My mind is still waking up, but I think I have an idea that might work."

As they neared the tree line, Alex reached for her hand. His fingers, icy from his time in the snow, wrapped around hers. She pulled back, surprised at the gesture, until she realized what Alex must be planning.

She was his new cover.

TWO

Alex slipped on a pair of nonprescription, black-framed glasses as they exited the cover of the woods. The athletic man who had been overly friendly to Violet narrowed his eyes at the sight of them. "Violet? Are you sure you're okay?"

"I'm Alex Ross." He reached out with his right hand to shake theirs. "Sorry if we scared you. I got into town late to meet Violet, but Teddy needed a walk before we went back inside." At the mention of his name, the giant dog leaned against Alex's legs and looked up. "Violet said you're Eryn and Bruce."

Eryn laughed. "And Teddy certainly knows you. Are you two...?"

"It's new," Violet said stiffly. Her hand

wrapped tighter around his. "Alex is from Utah."

Alex beamed. He hadn't had time to explain his intentions, but she *had* offered to help in any way she could. She obviously understood. Rick had always said Violet would be better at undercover work than either of them. Knowing her quick wit, Alex had never doubted it. "Long-distance relationships can be tricky, so we wanted to keep it low-key."

There was no one else in the world but Violet who wanted to get the Firecracker behind bars as badly as he did. Rick's death demanded justice. And while still a little groggy, he had realized she would be the best contact he had in town. This way, he could make sure she was safe and have a reason to catch up without attracting suspicion. Rick would've wanted him to make sure she was doing okay. Alex only regretted it'd taken him two years to do so.

"So, you're here on a short visit?" Bruce

made no effort at hiding the fact he was evaluating him, sizing up the competition.

"Might be doing a little job hunting, actually. I work in hospitality, so I might get a feel for the resort while I'm here."

"Where are you staying? Oh, never mind. That's a silly question." Eryn laughed, pointing at Violet. "Your mom must be glad someone will finally be staying in the vacation rental."

Violet had a rental? Alex simply smiled and nodded.

"Honey," Violet said slowly. Bruce pulled his chin back in surprise at Violet's use of the endearment. Alex tried not to enjoy the reaction. "It's getting cold," she said. "And late. Sorry to dash, Eryn, but maybe Bruce will keep you company the rest of the night? I'd like to catch up with Alex after his long drive here."

With a jolt, Alex realized he didn't see Violet's dress shoes or purse on her person. "Where's your purse?"

"Oh, I left it with Daniella."

Eryn squinted, a look of suspicion on her face, and addressed Alex. "You've heard about Daniella?"

"He knows I mentor her," Violet answered easily, tossing aside the test her friend seemed to have wanted Alex to fail. "I'll catch up with you later, Eryn." Violet tightened her grip on his hand and pulled him forward, gaining distance from her two friends. "I'll just grab my stuff, and we can walk to my house."

"You walked?"

"I actually came with Eryn, but I planned to walk home. It's not far. There's a walking path to the east of the river."

"In the dark, in the winter."

"With Teddy." He felt her fingers stiffen, no doubt with irritation. "You might have forgotten, but I'm a trained officer, Alex."

He bristled. "So am I, and they got the jump on me."

She dropped his hand as if it had burned her. They rounded the corner of the lodge.

"You're right. Being trained doesn't guarantee safety. For either of us."

She was referencing Rick's death. He struggled to find something to say, but she stopped in front of a podium that had a locked glass case over rows of keys. "The purse is gone."

Alex finally felt warmth in his fingers and toes, but not for good reason. If her purse was gone—

"Daniella?" Violet called out to the dark parking lot.

A teenager with long hair braided down her back appeared behind them with a steaming cup. "Sorry, Stephen got me some cocoa."

The purse and heels were dangling from Daniella's elbow. "I took them inside with me to make sure they'd be safe."

"That was very thoughtful. Thank you." Violet reached for the items.

"You had them with you the entire time?" Alex asked.

Daniella raised an eyebrow. "Well, I set

them down for a second. No offense, but a bunch of rich people aren't going to be tempted by Violet's stuff. Maybe the employees, but I kept a watch on them."

"I'm sure it's fine. Thank you." Violet eyed Alex warily as she leaned over and gave Daniella a quick hug.

Alex overheard Daniella whisper, "Who's the guy?"

"I'll tell you later," Violet replied with another whisper before ending the hug. Eryn and Bruce both passed them and re-entered the party, waving their goodbyes.

The faster he got the flash drive out of her purse, the better. They strode away from the lodge. "I'll drive you home," he said.

She opened the back door of his sedan, and Teddy made himself comfortable, taking up the entire three seats. She pointed to the passenger side. "Unless you're willing to call this in and find out what drug they gave you, I'm driving."

He'd call his handler later, but calling

for backup might ruin their chances of catching the Firecracker. They suspected someone on the target's security detail was helping the assassin.

"Whatever it was, I'm fine now." He tossed her the keys. "But I'm not arguing. You know the area better anyway."

They got in quickly, and she started the car. "I'm surprised Bruce and Eryn didn't recognize you, since you bumped into me at the party."

Alex reached into the console and pulled out his tablet. He slid the adapter into the side, preparing it for the flash drive. "People see what they expect to see." He grabbed the silver purse she'd set over the cup holders. "For instance, did you see I dropped a flash drive in your purse?"

Her eyes widened. "No."

He held up the purse for permission to rifle. She nodded and returned her attention to the road. "The flash drive is going to help you find the Firecracker?"

"Hopefully. There is more than one potential target at the resort this season—"

"Politicians and celebrities love this place."

"We think a member of the target's security detail put their itinerary on the flash drive and arranged it to be delivered to the Firecracker through a series of handoffs. I managed to switch it for my own with a tracking device." The evening bag opened with barely any effort, the magnetic clasp revealing sparse contents. "I put the drive with the itinerary in your purse in case the men found it on me. One look at the itinerary, and we should be able to figure out who Firecracker is targeting." He frowned. "There's hardly anything in here."

"Dress purses aren't designed with security in mind. My keys and wallet. That's it."

He dumped over the bag and let the two items fall onto the keyboard. "Unfortunately, you're right." His throat burned with sudden indigestion. No drive. Daniella must have set it down longer than she'd implied.

He hit the power on the tablet. He had one trick up his sleeve. "So they got their flash drive back. But maybe they still have the one I slipped them, too."

The tracking software flashed to life. The blinking dot moved along a road. He breathed a sigh of relief. "They're on the move."

Violet took a left turn.

The dot continued to move. "They just turned from Sunset Strip onto Serenade Lane."

"We're on Serenade Lane." Her voice had a monotone quality.

Alex strained forward. "Then we're gaining on them. Can you speed up?"

She pressed on the accelerator. "Alex?"

He focused on the map. Questions were going to have to wait. "Now they're on Cottonwood."

"Serenade turns into Cottonwood. Alex,"

she said more sternly. "There's no one but us on the street."

"Then we haven't spotted them yet. The dot is still moving."

She took a sharp turn and stopped. "Is it moving still?"

His irritation spiked. "What are you doing? They've turned on—" He pulled in a sharp breath. The dot had stopped moving, but how could that be? Violet grabbed her purse from him and rooted around in the bag. She frowned and unzipped a front pocket.

His veins felt like they were pumping lava as she held up a silver drive. The same flash drive he'd planted in the woman's clutch.

"Is it possible you made a mistake?" she asked.

He shook his head. "Even if I had— which I didn't—I dropped the flash drive in the main compartment. This was intentional."

"Then you're not the only one with sleight of hand."

His finger shook as he pointed to the front pocket. "Someone is sending me a message."

The Firecracker or his courier had not only seen Alex make the switch, they must have seen Violet, too. All thanks to Alex. He struggled to get the words he needed to say past the tightness in his throat. "Violet, I'm afraid I've put you in danger."

She gripped the steering wheel tightly, trying to absorb the information. Much about Rick's death was still a mystery to her. The scant details she'd obtained had been hard-earned by begging his supervisor, who'd held tears in his own eyes. What she *did* know was that Rick had been collateral damage when a bomb, intended for the Firecracker's target, went off early. She hadn't even been told who the original target was. The only other detail provided had been the assurance that Rick hadn't suffered.

Now the assassin who had killed her husband might have seen what she looked like. Maybe even knew her name? Good. Let the Firecracker understand who he'd hurt by taking Rick before his time. She blinked rapidly, surprised at her own reaction.

Teddy's nose touched her shoulder. The scientist had to be right. He could smell her emotions. Her heart was racing, but Teddy wasn't smelling fear. She couldn't tell Alex her thoughts, though. She'd sound like a maniac.

In danger? If the man wanted to kill her, let him try. Somewhere deep inside, she had always welcomed a chance to come face-to-face with Rick's killer. She'd been praying the same prayer for two years, two months and ten days. The words ran through her mind again, almost on autopilot.

Give me the grace to forgive the mur-

derer, but please give me the chance to see him brought to justice.

Alex studied her. "Violet?"

"I heard you." She offered him a smile. "Where are you staying?"

Alex didn't answer her. Instead, he opened the passenger door and stepped out.

"What are you doing?" Maybe she should've worried more about whatever they'd injected him with. "Alex, this is your car."

"You don't have to use your calm and coaxing voice. I'm fully aware. Just give me a second." He dropped the flash drive to the ground, lifted his foot, and struck the device with his heel. The strength and deliberate force smashed the casing, sending a plastic shard into the car. She flicked it off the passenger seat.

Alex picked up the debris and leaned into the vehicle to get a closer look at it under the dome light. "Need to make sure the circuit board is destroyed in case they made a clone or added their own tracker."

He returned to his seat and closed the door. "Let's go to your place," he said. "I imagine you have several questions, and since I dragged you into this, we need to make a plan. I'd like to see your security system before I call it a night."

She held her tongue even though he kept forgetting that she'd trained as a law enforcement officer, too. Rick had rarely been protective, perhaps because they'd studied together and entered law enforcement at the same time. Her husband had confidence in her abilities from their first day together. Alex didn't seem to share the sentiment.

The only security system she had was a doorbell camera and a few well-placed weapons throughout the house. Her phone was in her coat pocket, but the app would've vibrated had there been any movement near the house. She turned onto the side street leading up the steep hill to her place. "This is why I walk a lot of places."

"Not because you have a natural affinity for the forest?"

She tried to smile at his attempt at levity but wasn't in the mood. "Walking is often faster than using the roads around here, and it's beneficial for Teddy. The forest service manages most of the land surrounding the resort. The resort is within our district, licensed as a partnership. That's why our USFS building is on the main thoroughfare at the base of Ace Mountain."

Her place was set apart from the other houses and condominiums facing the River Run. Nestled into the side of the hill, this section of woods, west of Wood River, led to the Smoky Mountains.

Alex got out of the car after her and appraised the luxury cabin in front of him. Her portion of the building, designed to look like a ski chalet, had tall windows and a balcony that afforded her a gorgeous view of the buttes and peaks that weren't part of the resort. She spent most of her time traversing them with Teddy. Alone. Unless they were on a search-and-rescue mission, which happened more than she'd imagined when she'd moved here.

"I live on the top floor. The bottom level has a separate entrance. It's like two separate houses with a locked door keeping the levels apart. Safe. Especially since the ground floor is empty right now." The floodlights flashed on as she approached the wooden steps of the A-frame.

"You own this?"

"It's the rental Eryn was referring to. My mom actually owns the place. She handed it over to me when she moved to Boise."

"I'm surprised it's empty during peak season."

She snorted. "Not if you read the reviews." She looked down at Teddy by her side. "His middle name isn't Thunder for nothing." She laughed at the shocked look on his face. "I pay the full price for both floors. If I happen to rent out the bottom level, it goes in my pocket. I learned pretty fast that I prefer it empty." She trudged up the stairs. "Though it is nice to be able to offer it when someone really does need a place to stay."

"Like me?" They reached the top platform, and he handed her back her purse.

She lifted the keys out and inserted them into the lock. "Do you really need a place to stay, Alex?"

He tapped the camera placed next to her door, deftly avoiding her question. "Doesn't a camera light usually come on? A red light?"

She left the keys dangling and grabbed her phone. No notifications. Alex was right. Her phone should be chirping with their movements. Teddy's spine stiffened like when he caught a scent. He spun around in a circle, lifting his nose up and down. He touched his nose to the door, barked and then looked pointedly at Violet.

Alex flinched. "His bark sounds like a gunshot. Tired of being in the cold, huh, buddy?"

"Be glad he doesn't bark often." She tried to keep her voice light, but it trembled. Teddy's golden eyes told her everything she needed to know. She stepped to the side of the door so the window insert wouldn't reveal her location if anyone was still inside. She beckoned Alex. "Do you want to call the police, or is it still best to keep this to ourselves?"

"What is it? What did you see?"

"Teddy's reaction. He's found a scent that doesn't belong here. I think someone might be inside."

THREE

Alex pulled out his gun and scanned the still landscape before turning around. "Why don't you have your weapon out?"

"I didn't bring one."

"You didn't have a weapon when you went after me in the woods?"

"I had Teddy."

"He's not an attack dog." He pressed his lips together. They'd be having a conversation about that later. "Get behind me. I can't imagine the Firecracker could've beat us here, but if I'm mistaken again, I'll be the one paying the price. Are we clear? Stay behind me."

She tilted her head in confusion. "Again? I don't understand."

This wasn't the time to explain he was responsible for Rick's death. "I'm going in."

"You're not clearing the house alone. I have a gun in the back of the silverware drawer, next to the refrigerator."

"You stay behind me, and we'll go straight there. You're familiar with two-man entry?" He wasn't sure law enforcement rangers ever needed to practice such skills.

She rolled her eyes, disabusing him of that notion. "Of course. You clear the door."

He stepped to the other side of the entry and pointed the gun at a forty-five-degree angle. "Ready."

Violet twisted the key in the lock and shoved the door open, giving Alex a clear view of the kitchen and living room's open floor plan. He brought the gun up to chest level as he spun into the room. His gaze swept left to right. "Clear."

Teddy barreled into the room, almost knocking him over. The dog sniffed the floor with such intensity the area rug shifted. In his peripheral vision, Violet slipped past him. He heard the jarring of silverware and the click of a gun being readied to fire. Teddy grew more intent on sniffing the area in front of the armoire. Alex pointed at the hallway and dared a quick look over his shoulder. Violet nodded, her gun at the same forty-five-degree angle.

They worked in tandem, guarding each other's backs, keeping their guns at the ready as they cleared the hallway bathroom, a guest bedroom and, finally, the main bedroom and bath. At least the bedrooms had blinds and curtains, unlike the floor-to-ceiling windows in the living room.

"We need to check the bottom floor, as well. To be safe." Teddy barreled down the hallway. His paws slapped against the hardwood floors, and the sound of his journey echoed against the walls. "I guess I can stop whispering."

She shrugged but didn't lower her weapon fully. "Follow me." She exited the hallway and crossed the living room to a wooden door that had a deadbolt. Teddy sniffed the rug again and stood at attention at the armoire.

"What's in there? Could someone be hiding inside?"

"TV and some drawers below it."

A burglary didn't really seem likely. He'd passed a laptop on her desk in the main bedroom, and judging by dust patterns, the jewelry box on top of her dresser also didn't seem to have been disturbed. He held up a hand, and just to be sure, he flipped open the cabinet. There was a small flat screen television inside. He slid the drawers open and closed. Nothing except for what appeared to be a couple scraps of papers sliding around. He closed it back up. "Any cash hidden anywhere?"

"Very small amount in my fire safe, which I noticed is still on the floor of my closet. You said I might be in danger. Why are you asking about possible theft?"

"There wouldn't have been enough time from the moment you left your purse behind at the resort until now for the Firecracker to have located the house and left before we arrived."

Mere minutes. And even if the Firecracker had been here in Violet's home, what could he have hoped to achieve? Alex kept an eye out for any evidence of the assassin's signature bombs, but there was nothing. "Did you go straight to the dinner from here?"

"No. Eryn picked me up so we could get ready together. I was at her house for a couple of hours beforehand." She adjusted the grip on her weapon. "Continue the search?" At his nod, she flipped the bolt, and they took to the stairs. Teddy stayed upstairs as they searched the lower level, which eased his mind. Unlikely that any intruder had come downstairs, then.

Violet lowered her gun. "All clear."

"I'm going to do a quick check outside. And, I'd like to rent the place. What's your rate?" He nodded at the furnished living area. The resort was completely full, so he'd thought he was going to end up in a hole-in-the-wall thirty minutes away. This was much better, and he'd be able to keep an eye—or at least an ear out—for Violet's safety above.

"You were the brother Rick never had. You know we, I—" She exhaled after the correction. "I would never turn you away." She slipped her gun into her coat pocket. "I'll meet you upstairs to give you the keys." She pointed to the door. "This place has its own entrance."

He exited through the door she'd pointed out. The snow made quick work seeping into his socks and pants for the second time that night. He searched not only for any hidden explosives but also footprints. Nothing. Either Teddy was overreacting or a rodent had made its way into Violet's place. He grabbed his pack from the car and climbed the stairs again. His neck tingled at the doorbell camera. Still no red light at the movement. He gave the box a slight tug and the camera came out of its frame smoothly. The screws were missing, and the back indicated it was no longer plugged directly into the house.

Maybe Teddy deserved more credit. The question remained whether this was related to the Firecracker or an odd coincidence. Either way, he wasn't leaving until he was sure Violet was safe. He let himself in and locked the door behind him.

He set the camera on the counter. "Doesn't do much good without power."

"How'd they detach it without my notifications being set off? I've checked. No camera footage of anyone approaching."

"And nothing is missing in the house?"

"Nothing. I've double-checked. I suppose it's possible a thief tried to get in and couldn't. Doesn't explain Teddy's reaction to the rug, though." She flipped on the lights and pressed a button that lowered drapes over the glass wall. "It's a shame. I love stepping out to the sunlight in the morning."

He tapped the top of the camera. "This is all the security you have, isn't it?"

She offered him a sad smile. "I'm no longer a spouse of an FBI special agent. If you want to get technical, I'm not a law enforcement officer anymore, either. At least, I don't carry a badge. And I no longer live in a metro area. The camera and Teddy have been more than sufficient for the past couple of years."

"You're not still a ranger?" He'd spotted her USFS SUV out front, though.

"I'm the district ranger, responsible for all the employees who manage the three hundred thousand acres of land. It's a promotion of sorts. The law enforcement rangers are all out in the field and in partnership with the county sheriff. It's why I no longer carry a gun."

"Why the switch?"

She sighed, an indicator that it was a long story, best for another time. She crossed over to a kettle on the kitchen counter. "How about some tea?" She opened the fridge and produced two microwave meals. "And dinner. I didn't have a chance to eat."

A quick glance over her shoulder revealed eggs, bacon, Parmesan cheese and spinach. "You have spaghetti noodles?"

She quirked an eyebrow. "Yes." She pointed at a cabinet to her right.

"Then put those boxed atrocities away. We both deserve a *real* dinner after tonight." He stepped past her. "Might as well get comfortable. We at least need to discuss the short-term plan, starting with tomorrow." He pulled out the ingredients and a skillet and got to work on his fast and easy interpretation of spaghetti carbonara.

"I forgot you enjoyed cooking and being bossy, Alexander." Her teasing glint vanished. Her eyebrows shot up, and her mouth fell open slightly. If he hadn't understood why, he'd have been sure someone had punched her in the stomach. She blinked rapidly, spun away and walked down the hallway.

The memories came fast and furious. He'd teased Rick when he'd heard Violet call him Richard. She used Rick's full name whenever she got annoyed. Violet had responded to Alex's teasing by calling him by his full name, as well. That was probably the last time he'd seen Rick double over with laughter. Inside jokes without Rick here to laugh along with them...

Alex inhaled slowly and exhaled even slower. The pain in her eyes had matched his. Would either of them ever be able to be in the same room without the bitter reminder of what they'd lost?

Teddy brushed up against his legs, panting. "Smell the bacon, huh? Coming up shortly." He didn't make Teddy move as he worked. The weight and heat from the dog against his calves proved oddly comforting, better than a hug. No complicated sharing of feelings necessary.

A moment later, Violet reappeared in emerald green sweats with the US Forest Service logo embroidered on the shoulder. He truly looked at her for the first time tonight. Ironically, she seemed more fragile now than in her dress. Vulnerable.

The question in her eyes caused his neck to feel on fire. He was going to have to tell her. It was part of the reason he'd stayed away, but deep down, he knew he'd never have peace until he asked for forgiveness. The words were stuck in the back of his throat. *It should've been me. We traded places at the last minute. It was my call.* The splatter of hot bacon grease hit his wrist, slapping away the temptation.

"Let's start from the beginning." Violet poured herself a mug of hot water and added a tea bag. She propped her hip against the kitchen cabinet and watched him fry the pieces of bacon. "Why do you think the Firecracker is here?"

"Have you heard of the assassination market?"

"Dark web kind of thing." Her forehead wrinkled ever so slightly. "People make bets on powerful people dying on certain days. Horrible, but it's hard to investigate and prosecute."

"Yes. It's a hit list in disguise. The assassin essentially names his price, or bet, and picks the day or week that it will happen. Except sometimes there are even fewer details than a person's name. Sometimes it's a category like 'powerful political leader dies at a ski resort on vacation.'"

She set down the mug. "Rick thought the market had been defunct."

"The Bureau thought so, as well, until there was a huge cash out in bitcoins a few months ago. The market's still running, albeit harder to track. Do you know who is staying at the resort this season who could be a target?"

He'd never noticed before that her eyes got bluer when she was deep in thought.

"The governor of Idaho seems like a low-power target when I think about the Firecracker's profile," she said.

"Exactly why I'm asking. We can't rule him out, but there is likely a bigger target. We've checked the itineraries of senators and representatives. Nothing. Any ideas of other potential targets that might be here on vacation?"

"No. But I think I can find out."

Violet hung up as the call went to voice mail. Tom Curtis was the busiest man in the valley. He would know who was staying at the resort, the top names. His job was to keep the VIP customers happy, which usually involved the rich, famous and powerful. She had other contacts at the resort she could ask, but most of the famous guests used aliases to register their rooms. At least, according to Daniella, Tom's daughter, they did.

Alex placed heaps of pasta on a plate and handed it to her. "No news?"

"He's a hard guy to reach. We might have to go in person tomorrow night. He's always at the Waller Restaurant, an exclusive restaurant on the top floor of the resort's main hotel."

"How hard would it be to get a reservation? If I get eyes on potential targets and their security details, I might be able to figure this out and request backup."

She inhaled the heady aroma of bacon and Parmesan. "No. Reservations are impossible. Platinum-tier guests only. But…" She sighed. "I have a standing invitation on file for dinner. One I thought I'd never accept." Tom claimed Daniella had gotten her life back on track thanks to Violet. Although Violet disagreed, Tom insisted on thanking her by treating her like a VIP. She'd declined his offer of dinner at the Waller Restaurant, but he'd said her name would be always on the list. "They bring in celebrity chefs on a rotation. It's famous for food and live music, even though the restaurant doesn't technically exist."

Alex beamed. "We need to check it out, then." He picked up his own plate of food. "Guess we're about to have our first date." He winked but must have seen her sudden discomfort. "Bad joke. I'm sorry I dragged you into this."

"I would do *anything* to bring Rick's killer to justice, Alex." Her eyes stung. She crossed the room to the couch and took a seat. "Sorry. My table is still in storage. I don't entertain much anymore."

He crossed the room to sit on the opposite side of her. "I should've asked. Are you already dating someone?"

She laughed. "No. Not even remotely interested. No offense to your choice of cover." She took a bite and let the flavors swirl around her mouth. The man really could cook.

"I was still a little groggy when I made that decision. I should've clued you in, but you picked up my intentions immediately. That's great undercover instinct. You can tell your friends our relationship is much less serious than I implied."

"My friends mean well, but they've been relentless in trying to fix me up lately. It's not that I'm against..." She exhaled, searching for the right words. "I miss sharing life with someone, but no one can be Rick. So why try?" She shrugged. "I guess that means serving as your cover is a win-win for me."

"Win-win? How do you figure?"

She hadn't meant to give him so much insight into her grieving. "You asked why I switched jobs. The experts say not to make big changes after a loved one's death, so I tried going back to work. But on every case, I wanted the suspect to be Rick's killer. It messed with my mind. I no longer trusted my judgment. Teddy picked up on it, too. He started acting confused by my commands. So I decided to throw away the rule book on grieving and change everything all at once. I moved back here and took the district ranger position. It helped. Some. But if my friends stop playing matchmaker because they think I'm taken and I also play a small part in helping take down Rick's killer..."

"Ah. That's what you meant by win-win. Once we get the Firecracker, will you go back into law enforcement?"

"I'm not sure about that. Either way, I think I'd have peace that at least I tried. Having a background in law enforcement and not being able to..." Her voice shook with the frustration that she'd tamped down for years.

"I miss him, too." His fingers fidgeted with the edge of the afghan resting on the back of the couch. "It's why I switched to undercover work. I want to find the Firecracker, sure, but I'm also not ready for another partner." His voice had a gruff texture that wasn't there before.

Violet knew if she wanted, they could reminisce in a way that no one else could. The thought terrified her.

He set down his plate on the end table and strode toward the corner where Teddy now rested on his dog bed. "Interesting decor you've got here." The change of subject was a relief, and it probably meant Alex wasn't ready to reminisce, either.

She laughed and popped up on her knees to view the area behind the couch, as well. She'd used her favorite frames that had once held photos of her and Rick to fill with photos of other Newfoundland dogs. "It's our inspiration wall." Teddy released a grumbling noise.

"He doesn't sound inspired. This one is just a photo of a statue."

She scoffed. "He's tired. So am I. That's a statue of Sergeant Gander, in Canada. Yes, a dog," she clarified to Alex's raised eyebrows. "World War II hero. A grenade landed near the wounded soldiers. He picked it up and ran it toward the enemy." She pointed at the next one. It featured a black-and-white dog mid-dive. "That's Whizz. He saved hundreds of lives as a marine rescue dog. Then, you have an illustration of the nanny from Peter Pan, and the final one is the dog that accompanied Lewis and Clark. All Newfoundland dogs."

Teddy grumbled again. Odd. Maybe he wasn't just tired. "What is it?" The dog jumped up and went to the armoire again. This time, with the lights on, she noted his spine was stiff. "He's found that same scent again." She got off the couch and walked forward. "Whoever messed with the security camera definitely got inside and spent a lot of time here."

Her skin electrified at the thought of an intruder focusing on the armoire. There was nothing inside but the television and drawers filled with Rick's personal items. Photographs, yearbooks, medals, memorabilia, things that had made him laugh were all stored in there. Nothing of value except to her. Actually, that reminded her there was something in there Rick probably would want Alex to have. She reached out—

"Don't!" Alex crossed the room. "I should've checked behind and underneath before disregarding Teddy's reaction. If the Firecracker—"

"The Firecracker has no reason to kill me, and you said it yourself, there wasn't enough time between the flash drive drop and coming back here. This has to be unrelated."

He didn't answer but took a knee. "Nothing behind here. Let me check one more thing." He got on all fours, and Teddy's head disappeared underneath the armoire along with him. "No, no kisses. Teddy, please."

She fought back a laugh. "You can't get on his level without expecting affection. Can I open it now?"

Alex reappeared, wiping his cheek off. "I suppose it's safe. I opened it once before in the dark. Nothing happened then." Teddy pulled his head back from underneath, as well.

"Okay, boy. Show me what's bothering you." She opened the door. Teddy pressed his nose against the three drawers. One drawer at a time. Her insides felt full of hot lava. "Teddy, sit," she whispered. Her fingers refused her internal demand to remain calm and trembled as she pulled open the first drawer.

Gone. Empty. "Someone took it." Her breath grew shallow and rapid. "Rick's photos." She grabbed the second drawer. Dust. Nothing but dust. "His yearbooks and medals." Her voice hitched.

Alex moved past Teddy at her side. "I thought they were supposed to be empty. I didn't know." He reached over and pulled the third drawer before she could.

Her favorite wedding photo, ripped in two, spun in opposite directions at the sudden motion. Rick's face had a red line drawn through it. A cry lodged in her throat. Alex reached for the second half of the photograph. Violet's face had a red circle around it, but no line.

He straightened and reached for her hand, but she seemed to have gone numb, because she felt nothing but the roaring in her head.

"Violet..." His forehead tightened.

She said the words both of them had to be thinking. "It means I'm next."

FOUR

Alex was a light sleeper on a normal night. After the events of last night, he hardly slept at all. When he did catch a few minutes, his dreams were fueled by memories of Rick looking over his shoulder and saying "I need to talk to you after this. Something about this is starting to seem familiar." The dream always ended with Alex staring at a ball of fire, knowing that his partner was gone.

He sat up straight, sweat rolling down his neck. It was the fourth time in one night that he'd woken up from the same dream. Probably natural given the nature of the case and the time he'd spent with Violet. None of it made sense, though. Sunlight streamed through the blinds.

He'd ended up sleeping later than he thought.

Thumping above followed by the sounds of grunts sent him flying out of bed. Those were sounds of a scuffle. Violet was being attacked. He ran barefoot in his navy sweats up the stairs to the connecting door. He grabbed the knob, but it didn't budge. Locked. He didn't think she would lock him out. He pounded on the door. More thumping and grunts could be heard. The small landing with a thin balcony rail prevented him from taking a run at the door.

He descended two stairs at a time and raced for his exit, slipping on his shoes without socks and grabbing his coat. He pulled it on as he ran, arriving at the front entrance to her level within seconds. Also locked. The drapes on the windows were still shaded. Teddy jumped up on the glass insert and barked.

Alex pounded. "Violet! If you're okay in there, I need you to open up in ten seconds, or I'm going to break through. Teddy, move!"

His fingers twitched, tempted to grab his gun and shoot the door down, but Teddy might get hurt. Alex stepped back on the wooden deck. He had room for a running start. This particular door looked most vulnerable at its hinges.

An engine revved up the hill behind him. A silver Jeep pulled up behind Alex's car. Bruce, the so-called friend from last night, stepped out of the vehicle. "She kick you out?" Bruce asked, laughing.

Just great. He didn't have time to explain.

"Alex, was it?"

He ignored Bruce, taking one more step back and focusing hard on the spot he was about to kick.

The door flung open. "What?" Violet's eyes were wide, and her hair was dripping with sweat. "What is it?" She swung her gaze to the driveway. "Bruce?"

Alex fought down irritation, panting

from the adrenaline, and turned to Bruce. "One second, please. I need a word with Violet."

She tilted her head, frowning, but opened the door wide for him. He stepped inside. "You're okay? I heard fighting."

"Fighting? I told you Teddy can be loud when he walks around."

"This was more than Teddy. Thumping, sure, but grunting, fast feet. It sounded like you were fighting off..." He let his words trail off as her face turned a brighter shade of red.

She held a hand to her forehead. "I'm sorry. I thought I was being quiet. Didn't realize sound carried so well down there."

"Quiet about what?"

"Tang Soo Do. It's a martial art. Teddy likes to think he can do the forms, too, so he jumps around a lot. I didn't think you could hear me."

"Practicing forms doesn't usually sound like you're hitting something."

"I have padded targets for practice." She

offered a sheepish laugh. "Guess the vacation reviews really do have merit. The floor must not have good insulation. I'm sorry if I worried you."

He blew out a breath. "It's fine. I didn't know that was your thing. New?"

"No. Though I took a break from it for a while. Do you still pitch?"

Alex pulled back in surprise. He'd gone to school on a baseball scholarship, and despite an offer to the minors, he'd decided to follow in his family's footsteps and pursue a career in criminal justice. "You knew about that?"

"Rick bragged that you ensured the FBI softball team won every game."

"Yeah, well, I'm still on a break. Haven't pitched since I went into undercover work."

The light in her eyes dimmed, but she nodded. "Well, again, I'm sorry to have scared you."

Bruce stepped inside, not waiting for an invitation. If she hadn't called the man a friend, Alex would have something to say.

"Everything okay?" Bruce held a white sack with a bakery logo stamped on the front and a bouquet of dahlias.

"Yes, of course." Violet gestured at herself. "I'm afraid I'm not ready to entertain right now."

"Oh, I don't mind." Bruce set the bag and flowers on the counter. "I brought you some muffins." He darted a glance at Alex. "I was hoping to have a word with you alone, as well, Violet."

Alex crossed over to the cabinet, where he picked out a coffee mug and poured himself a cup of coffee from the hot carafe. He needed it more than ever. He turned around and blew on his coffee. "Oh, don't mind me. Go ahead."

Bruce narrowed his eyes while Violet smirked, clearly amused. The man shuffled his feet and stuck his hands in his coat pockets. He leaned forward, leaving very little room between him and Violet.

Teddy barreled in between them, threw his front paws on the counter and grabbed the bag of muffins. He ran past them to his bed.

"What kind of muffins were those?" Violet asked, alarmed.

Alex set down his mug and pulled out the treat he had in his coat pocket. He had intended to give it to Teddy when he came to see them after the case. That reminded him that he'd never found out why Violet had been at the party last night in the first place.

Alex whistled while he removed the cellophane wrapping of the meat stick. Teddy dropped the muffin bag and ran, sliding into a sitting position when his front paws reached Alex's feet. "Good dog." He dropped the treat in Teddy's mouth.

Violet jogged over to retrieve the bag and beamed. "Thank you, Alex."

"I thought he was well trained," Bruce objected.

"Highly," Violet said. "When he knows he's on the job. But he's still a dog." She pulled his food bin out of the pantry. "I got a late start this morning. He counter-surfs if I get behind schedule."

"Can you blame him?" Alex said, unable to keep the grin off his face. He picked up his mug again and took a sip. Bruce looked livid.

"What did you want to talk about, Bruce?" Violet shot Alex a look that seemed to tell him to behave.

"I—I just wanted to make sure you were okay. Eryn and I were talking last night, and…" Bruce leveled a narrowed gaze at Alex. "You never know with internet dating if people are really who they claim to be." He plastered a fake smile on his face. "No offense, man."

"None taken."

"I never said we met on the internet." She smiled but didn't offer any other information.

The man's neck turned another shade of

red during the awkward silence. "Sorry. I assumed that was the case since you never mentioned him to Eryn."

Ah, so Bruce was fishing for information, and Violet offered no indication she planned to give it. Alex made a circle motion with his hand, and Teddy, now done with his treat, flopped over on his back so Alex could give him a good tummy rub.

Violet laughed at the dog's antics. "As you can see, Alex and I know each other well, but I appreciate the concern. Thanks for stopping by. I really need to get to work now."

Bruce raised his left eyebrow and turned to Alex. "And you're spending the day out looking for a job?"

"Shadowing Violet, actually. Thought it'd be the best way to get to know the area. Well, that and taking her to the Waller Restaurant tonight." He might've gone too far, judging by the way the vein in Bruce's temple appeared ready to pop.

"The Waller Restaurant?" Bruce repeated, likely soaking in that Alex might be serious competition if he was taking her to the exclusive restaurant. "I'll call you later then, Violet." He gave Alex a quick, challenging glance before he left.

"Wow." Alex lifted the edge of the window coverings and watched Bruce get back in his vehicle. "He's aggressive."

Violet finished pouring Teddy's food into his bowl. "Most competitive person I know. Guess this cover isn't all bad." She straightened, her hands on her hips. "I'm carrying my gun today. Are you really coming to work with me, Alexander?"

At the use of his full name, he held out his hands in surrender. "Okay, I know interrupting your routine must be irritating, but humor me, please. I'll stay out of your hair, but I'd like to check the security of your office. It is my specialty. I also need to know why you were at the party last night."

She crossed the room and opened the drawer next to the silverware. "I was invited. Didn't think I'd go, but then Eryn really needed a night out."

"So, Eryn was the one that paid the two thousand dollars a plate?"

Violet guffawed. "Absolutely not." She pulled out a cardstock invitation and held it out to him. "We both got an invitation like this. 'Come honor the Governor of Idaho.'" She frowned. "It does seem like an odd thing if I stop and think about it, but we thought it was a local event. Two thousand a plate?" She shook her head. "Could it be that locals were invited for free and only nonresidents had to pay?"

Unlikely, but Alex didn't have any theories at the moment. Now that Bruce was gone, he noticed Violet's red-rimmed eyes for the first time. She'd cried last night. "There should be a fundraising paper trail," he said gently. "We can find out."

She poured herself a mug of coffee. "That's got to be what happened. There's no other explanation. Tom Curtis was in charge of the event. We could ask him tonight." She walked down the hallway. "I'm getting ready. You should, too, if you're really shadowing me."

Alex stared into his swirling coffee, processing the information. She'd received a personal threat—as personal as a threat could be. This changed everything. He'd never forget the look on her face after seeing her wedding photo desecrated. The target on Rick's face had to be the work of the Firecracker, but it didn't make sense. What possible reason could he have for targeting Violet on purpose? The invitation, the door camera, taking all of Rick's personal mementos...

None of that fit with the dossier the Bureau had built on the Firecracker. Whatever this was had a personal edge. Teddy pawed his sneaker, likely hoping for another treat. Alex stared into the dog's golden eyes as his own dilemma came into clear focus. He lifted up a silent prayer, hoping that he wouldn't be forced to choose between catching the Firecracker and keeping Violet safe. Violet's safety was top priority, but would she ever forgive him if he let Rick's killer slip through his fingers again?

Violet zipped up her evergreen work jacket and clipped Teddy's K-9 vest around his chest and back before they left. Alex waited outside his vehicle.

"You really don't have to come to work with me. I'm sure you have plenty to investigate on your own."

"It's what a good boyfriend who came to visit would do." He winked and moved to open the passenger door.

Her stomach fluttered from the flirtatious gesture, even though she knew he was only playing a part to keep up his cover. Such an odd sensation, especially since she'd never ever seen Alex as more than Rick's partner. Had he always been so attractive? Best not to think about it. She reached down and patted

Teddy's head. "If you're coming with me to work, we all go in my vehicle." She gestured at the white SUV with the forest service logo on the driver's side door. "The back half is outfitted for Teddy's needs. Temperature alarms, fans, even a heated water bowl."

Alex got into the passenger side of the vehicle. He wanted to talk about the photo they'd discovered last night. She could tell by his frequent side-glances and the way he kept taking big breaths and then closing his mouth. The only way to stay strong was to keep busy, to focus on what mattered.

If Rick were still alive, he would be making the world a better place. She felt the burden to do doubly as much in honor of him. That's why she put in long hours and volunteered. Her work saved lives, and she preferred to stay busy. Rarely was there a free evening like last night where she had time to socialize and think. The holidays stank in that regard. Silent nights were the worst.

"I feel safe here, despite what happened yesterday," she said. "I appreciate your protective nature. I know it comes naturally in your line of work, but it's not necessary." The sun reflected off the two-feet-high snowpack on either side of the road as she made her way down the hill to the town. "Besides, you don't think the Firecracker was in my house. It's probably some two-bit criminal that I or Rick put away. Teddy and I will catch him."

"I can't rule out any possibilities. I've already asked the Bureau to cross-reference any criminals in the area that might've been recently released from cases you or Rick worked on. Want to tell me any more about Bruce?"

"There's nothing to tell, because I'm not interested in him, and he's not a threat." He was recently divorced and seemed to be trying to reclaim his youth. She doubted he had any genuine interest in her, and he especially wouldn't when he realized she wasn't the same Violet he'd once known. "Haven't you had a relationship you regretted?"

"How many dates does it take to qualify as a relationship?"

"If you have to ask, you've never been in one."

"There you go, then." He tapped on his phone, searching for something. She wondered if he was finding anything surprising about Bruce after all. He shifted uncomfortably, adjusting the tight seat belt off his neck. "How's your family? In Boise now, right?"

She tightened her grip on the steering wheel. "My family is doing well." Her mouth dropped when she realized the significance of his question. Alex used to spend a lot of holidays with her and Rick in Utah. They'd always invited her sister, Dawn, to come, as well. "You really want to know about Dawn, don't you? Alex, I hate to be the one to break it to you." She cringed. "Dawn got married this year. Six months ago."

Alex shrugged. "I'm happy for her."

She pulled up to a stop sign and sneaked a peek at his face. Why did it bother her so much that Alex was alone? Many single people had full lives, herself included.

"You can stop with the looks of pity, Violet." He shook his head. "There were never any sparks with Dawn. Honest! On either side, despite what you and Rick wanted." His deep chuckle finally convinced her.

"Well, you couldn't blame us for trying." She made the final turn to the main road, now in the valley. "The double dates would've been such fun." Her voice shook ever so slightly. Caught off guard by the sudden wave of emotion, she faked a smile.

Every question meant to keep the conversation safe brought them back to Rick. The last couple of years, he'd slowly become a taboo subject. Friends and family stopped mentioning his name for fear she'd cry. And now, with Alex, they were talking about him every other minute. She hadn't realized how badly she'd needed to speak and hear his name.

"I'm a little surprised you didn't move to Boise after your mom and Dawn moved there. Didn't you come back here to be near them?"

"At first, yes. It wasn't a conscious decision, but since my mom lost my dad so many years ago, I thought she would be able to help me. I put too many expectations on her, that she would do the work of grieving for me."

He barked a laugh. "Moms are pretty good at fixing things, but not sure she could do that for you."

"Exactly. Being with me while I was so raw was too much for her. Seven years had gone by since we'd lost my dad, and she'd just started to date again. It was only six months after Rick's death that she told me it was time for *me* to get my nails and hair done and find a man."

"I don't imagine that went over well."

She laughed at the memory, even though at the time, she'd been livid. "Let's just say we have a more loving relationship when we live apart. I didn't understand how much work grief takes. Now we'd probably be fine in the same town. We visit each other often."

"I'm glad. I didn't mean to get so personal."

"It's okay. I know you were trying to make polite conversation before getting to the hard questions."

He slapped his knee and shook his head. "Nothing gets past you."

"How's your family doing?" she asked, knowing she sported a giant grin.

"Fine. All serving in public service all over the country and around the world. Same as always. Violet, I really do need to ask—"

"You want to know more about what

was taken from the armoire." She'd been prepared for this bit at least. "Everything from the years I knew him. When I moved here, I put most of the stuff from our house in storage, but there were certain things I wanted to keep near me. College yearbooks, photos, notes we shared, that kind of thing. His mother still has all his childhood stuff."

"College yearbooks? You guys met at college?"

"Yes. At a movie night in the dorms. We knew of each other from classes before then, as well, but we'd never really talked until that night. He was actually dating my roommate, Bridget Preston." Her name rolled off the tongue. "She had a magnetic personality. Drew in everyone until you got to know her better. The silent treatment and passive aggression were her tried-and-true methods, but you'd never know what you said or did to cause any of her moods."

She shook her head with the memories

as they came fast and furious. "Anyway, she didn't show that night, so Rick sat by me, and we really talked for the first time. That was all. She got wind and was enraged, even though we didn't even share popcorn."

"And she was your roommate? Hard to imagine Rick dating someone like that."

Alex's question reminded her of all the times she'd needed to sleep on the floor of another friend's dorm because she'd felt like she couldn't relax around Bridget's mood swings. Violet pulled into the parking lot.

"She was the definition of *charismatic*, so I don't blame Rick for being pulled in at first. I even managed to convince myself she was my best friend for a short while. We were both from Idaho. Both majoring in criminal justice. The following year, we were still roommates, but in a shared suite. She started a study group on criminal profiling. We studied most-wanted fugitives from case files our professor gave us. That's when I really started to get to know Rick. We were certain we had fresh insight that might break the cases open."

"Rick was in the study group? Was it kind of like that group of retired detectives in New York that try to solve cold cases over lunch?"

"Exactly, except without any experience. Rick started to feel like Bridget was more in awe of criminals than wanting to catch them. Anyway, he broke up with her before second semester, and Bridget decided it was because of me. So she framed me for plagiarism."

Alex's mouth dropped. "That's usually grounds for expulsion."

"Her intention. She turned in a plagiarized paper with my name on it. Artfully done, I might add. But Rick proved Bridget framed me."

"Hold up." He tapped on his phone.

"Don't bother." She glanced over his shoulder and confirmed her suspicions.

"Bridget isn't targeting me. She died a few years back."

Alex froze with his finger hovering over the headline he'd found. She knew what it said. A car crash had sent Bridget's vehicle over the edge of a cliff into Snake River Canyon.

"Rick and I were, in a weird way, thankful for her. She wanted to harm us, but instead, we gained each other." The words reminded her of a Bible verse, but the exact wording escaped her as a small red dot flickered on the dashboard and disappeared.

"Did you see that?" She spun to look over her shoulder, out the back window. Trees surrounded the parking lot of the district office. There was no sign of anyone, though.

"Violet?"

It wasn't a laser scope. It was more likely a reflection from a passing car. All this talk was making her brain susceptible to thoughts of danger. "Nothing," she said, searching again to be sure. The district office parking lot was just off Main Street, but the back end was set in one of the many areas of the national forest that wove throughout the resort area.

Alex scanned for threats as she helped Teddy out of the vehicle, and they entered the offices. Daniella, her mentee and volunteer, had already opened the office and was accepting calls from the public. The young adult gaped at Alex and gave Violet meaningful looks, complete with waggling eyebrows.

"This is my friend Alex. You might remember him from last night."

Daniella's expression as she waved at Alex made it clear she didn't believe he was only a friend. When Alex wasn't looking, Daniella opened her mouth wide and gestured at her shoulder, indicating she thought he was attractive.

Violet tried not to openly laugh. Daniella was so expressive, she made it clear to everyone what she was thinking. Violet checked messages and her schedule at her standing desk while Teddy found his bed behind it and made himself comfortable.

Alex pointed through the windows at the separate garage. "What's in there?"

"Storage and supplies. Extra snowmobiles, ATVs, ammunition and explosives."

His eyebrows jumped. "Explosives?"

"Avalanche mitigation. We make them happen safely before they block highways or put anyone in danger. If the conditions are ripe, recreationists can accidentally initiate them. Don't worry. The explosives are in a separate safe."

Daniella put down the phone. "Sheriff Bartlett is on the line for you. I've transferred the call to your desk."

Violet picked up the phone, not particularly bothered. If it was urgent or a search-and-rescue mission, she would've gotten an alert on her cell. She answered, and the sheriff plowed ahead.

"This is a courtesy call, nothing official, but your friend Eryn Lane is missing. She didn't show up to pick up her kid after morning preschool, apparently. Someone found a spilled coffee cup next to her vehicle on Wood River Avenue. It's not suspicious enough to call in a team yet, but I thought you should know. I've got my hands full now. Talk later." He hung up before she could ask one of a million questions swirling through her mind.

"What? What is it?" Alex stepped in front of her desk.

The red dot she'd seen before flashed on the back wall and moved swiftly to the center of Alex's chest. That was no reflection. "Get down!" He dropped into a crouch, and the red dot swung to Daniella. "Get under the desk!" The teenager dived without hesitation.

The dot disappeared. Her heart rate roared in her ears. What was going on? "I thought I saw a laser scope. Did you see it?"

Alex crawled to the window and looked out. "I didn't see anything, but I believe you. Though if we're really dealing with a sniper, they don't usually use lasers."

"Oh, that's reassuring," Daniella snapped from underneath the desk. "I didn't see it, either, though. Is it still there?"

Was she losing her mind? "No. Not anymore."

Alex pointed to the right. "I'm taking the back door. You up for taking the front? Sweep the area and meet me back in here."

They shifted into position, careful to avoid the windows. "Daniella, I need you to stay down until we're clear," she said. "No matter what. If you hear anything, call it in. Teddy, find Daniella." Teddy ran across the room, making his large form fit in the small space between Daniella and the desk legs.

"No kisses, Teddy!" Daniella objected, but Violet didn't hear the rest. The blood pounded in her ears as she swung the door open and scanned the trees. Every step over the pea gravel shot adrenaline up her spine.

"Violet!" Alex's voice rang out.

She sprinted with her hand on her weapon toward Alex's location back behind the garage. He stood to the east, pointing at thick tracks in the mud. The markings indicated someone had come close and turned around and left. "I think the threat is gone, but maybe it's time for us to see if Teddy can catch a scent?"

She felt pulled in different directions. "I'll call in my rangers to investigate. Teddy and I need to find Eryn first. She's my best and longest friend in the world, and the sheriff said she's missing. I'll never forgive myself if anything happens to her."

His eyebrows jumped. "I know the feeling better than most. And right now, I'm worried that something could happen to you. Where you go, I go."

"Then we better work fast." She turned

and ran to retrieve Teddy, trying to ignore the way her heart pounded in response to Alex keeping pace at her side.

FIVE

So much for working fast. Violet insisted on dropping Daniella off at home to make sure she was safe. Daniella took advantage of the time to ask how they knew each other and if the town rumors about their dating were true. The young woman had received a few informative text messages while waiting underneath the desk and knew all about their upcoming dinner that night. She could have a future in interrogation methods, and it was clear Violet wasn't used to telling her the bare minimum.

Now Alex tried not to let his impatience show as Violet held the empty coffee cup to Teddy's nose before he walked around Eryn's vehicle three times. At this rate, they'd lose the scent back at the forest service and risk losing their coveted reservation at the exclusive restaurant.

Working several cases at the same time wasn't unusual, but the importance of these two circumstances resulted in a painful knot behind his shoulder blade.

"Sometimes it takes him a bit to find it," Violet explained. "Especially if the scent has been compromised by a lot of people." Teddy's head snapped up, and he turned around and looked directly at Alex. He surged forward, headed directly for him and swerved at the last minute into the forested park across from the coffee shop.

"Good boy," she called. They jogged for several minutes until Teddy stopped, sniffing around. Violet took a deep inhalation but appeared shaky.

"Are you okay?"

"The work can be slow, tedious. It's why we train day in and out. We easily go eight or more miles on a search some days, but..."

"Eryn is your friend."

"Best." The word came out in a whisper. She blinked until her eyes no longer had a watery sheen. Alex hated she was out here. The left-behind cup of coffee was suspicious, but it could be a coincidence. Violet had already lost the love of her life, and now her friend had the nerve to get herself lost where most of the forest and mountain was without cell signal. Getting mad wouldn't be of any help, so he did the only other thing he could think of. Keeping her mind off worst-case scenarios was important. "Why'd you go into search and rescue?"

She pulled her chin back in surprise. "Rick never told you?" He shook his head and trudged after Teddy, who had his nose buried in the snow, apparently debating on where to turn now. "My great-grandfather got confused and walked into a snowstorm. They didn't find him in time. If there had been a search-and-rescue dog in that area, I feel certain tragedy could've been avoided."

"Wow." The change of subject definitely didn't lighten her mood. "And that's exactly what you're doing. Making sure Eryn's story doesn't end like that. You know she probably just wanted some time to herself and forgot to pick up her kid? I'm sure she's fine."

"That would be very unlike her." Violet kept her eyes on Teddy as they took a sharp turn left and began trudging along the bank of a river. "I actually wanted to start my own search-and-rescue school, but plans changed. Do you like undercover work?"

He laughed, taken off guard by the sudden change in subject. "I guess I don't enjoy adrenaline as much as some. The short answer is no."

"And the long answer? It's just us and the trees right now. We might be out here all day or until I can convince the sheriff to enlist the rest of the search-and-rescue team without waiting forty-eight hours."

He sighed. "Undercover agents have to find what's attractive about the choices criminals make so we can fit in better with them."

Violet's face broke into a smile, and he suddenly felt less cold, trudging in the deep snow. "I can't see you being good at that."

"People can tell when you don't approve of their choices. Wouldn't surprise me if Teddy can smell someone's being disingenuous. I keep finding myself having the same discussion while I'm undercover."

She stopped for half a second and turned to him. "You try to talk them out of their life of crime before you bring the whole operation down. Don't you?"

He rallied his best acting skills in hopes of keeping his neck from turning beet red and shrugged instead. "I may casually point out what else they'd be really good at. Guess it helps ease my conscience. But so far, it's only ever resulted in them doubling down on their criminal activities."

"Does that make the arrests easier?"

"Yes and no. The mission of the FBI is to protect the American people and uphold the Constitution. I can find peace that I've done my job. But I do get tired of hearing all the reasons why their choices are the best way, hearing them disregard the damage they've done to their own lives and the pain they've caused others."

"You have a good heart, Alex." Her warm smile, her bright eyes and the way she said his name all snapped something inside him, and his chest grew warm. He felt unsteady on his feet for half a second.

Rick's words the week before his death replayed in his head. *They say the most successful agents are the ones that have a solid support, a family to come home to at night. Maybe it's time to look at getting yourself that, Alex.*

His mouth went dry. Why was that memory choosing *now* to resurface? He'd only ever thought of Violet as Rick's wife, a friend, a wannabe matchmaker.

Her shoulders dropped. "Teddy's lost the scent, but he's trying to find it again." They trudged in silence for a few minutes until Teddy's tail straightened, and he launched out of sight. "I think he's got it again. Let's pick up the pace."

Teddy barked, and Violet bolted into action. She was sure-footed, while Alex clumsily fought to keep from falling on his face. He had to lift his knees high to run in the deep snow. Maybe he should train in the forest occasionally instead of his daily routine of three miles on sidewalks and pavement.

She passed a wrought iron bridge and suddenly disappeared. "Eryn!"

Alex made it past the bridge and slid down the muddy bank, absent from snow due to the overhead supports. Underneath, Violet was bent over, an ear on Eryn's chest.

"She's breathing. Heartbeat slow but

steady. Call 9-1-1. Tell them to send an ambulance to the Bow Bridge."

Alex didn't hesitate, and the moment he was off the call, he realized Teddy sat at attention, a chew toy in his mouth. The dog would need a bath. Mud coated the bottom of his tail as it swished in the muck.

Violet tapped Eryn's cheek, which was also coated in grime. "Wake up, Eryn. I need you to open your eyes." Eryn groaned, but her eyes didn't budge.

"She's been drugged." Just like the two men had tried to do to him. Maybe he was wrong, but his gut wouldn't let the idea go. The rocks behind Teddy extended for a good six feet before the water's edge. The river was maybe twenty feet across before reaching the rocky bank on the other side. "Is the water low enough to cross on foot?"

Violet worked her arm underneath Eryn's shoulders and began lifting her to a sitting position. "Yes. It's part of the irrigation system. The dam opens up in the spring. When it's at peak flow, the river reaches the top of the bank. Eryn, honey, wake up."

Far off, sirens accompanied the sound of water slapping the rocks. He looked in the direction they'd come. "Could we have gone down this bank earlier? Walked along the rocks this whole time?"

"I suppose. Eryn?"

Her friend groaned again and began blinking her eyes. Violet blew out a breath with a nervous laugh. "Are you okay?"

The woman's bloodshot eyes glanced around, and her face morphed into concern. "Where am I?" She cringed and placed a hand on the back of her head.

"Someone call 9-1-1?" a voice in the distance shouted.

"Down here," Alex hollered. A moment later, the EMTs slid their way down the mud underneath the bridge until they got to the rocks. The sheriff was right behind them as they took over caring for Eryn.

Alex barely registered the questions the sheriff and EMTs asked as he gazed over the area. Whoever drugged Eryn had been careful not to leave tracks in the muddy spots. Perhaps they'd made their way along the rocks instead. But why? The two men at the political party had tried to drug him, but he had thought it was about the flash drive. Was it possible Eryn was tied to the assassin or his target? She'd been the one to convince Violet to come to the party.

He turned to look at Violet's best friend with new perspective just as the sheriff remarked. "That's a whole lot of jewelry on your person, Miss Lane." The sheriff picked up her purse. "And a whole lot pouring out of your bag, as well."

The EMTs ignored the statement and placed Eryn on a stretcher.

"What are you talking about?" Eryn asked. "My kids…"

"They're with your husband," the sheriff said.

"We're separated." Eryn shook her head as if trying to shake free of the fog that Alex knew she had to be feeling. "You're right. He's still my husband."

"We need to ask you some questions regarding the theft that took place at the jewelry store."

"Sheriff." Violet stepped in between the man and her friend. "I don't appreciate the direction of these questions. Eryn's been drugged and very obviously framed."

"Excuse me, Ranger Sharp, but her vehicle was spotted at the scene by security cameras, and a woman matching Eryn's description, albeit wearing a mask, cleared the place out. Unless we discover that this jewelry is truly hers—"

"I've never seen it before." Eryn began to tremble. "Violet, what's going on? I don't even know how I got here!"

Violet squeezed her hand. "Don't worry. We're going to get this sorted out."

The EMT threw a blanket over her.

"We're taking her to the hospital now, Sheriff."

"Make sure you get a toxicology report," Alex interjected.

The sheriff turned to him, his left eyebrow raised. "Aren't you the new boyfriend in town? Who works in the hospitality industry? Mind telling me what makes you think—"

"Because I said she was drugged," Violet said, eyes wide. "And he's right. Order one." She nodded at the EMTs. They counted and lifted Eryn from both sides before they carried her up the side of the bank. Alex knew small-town gossip traveled fast, but for the sheriff to already know he was "the new boyfriend" was impressive.

"This isn't federal property, Violet," the sheriff said, his voice softer. Apparently, he only referred to her by her title when it suited him.

"Please. Let's not get into a turf war. You told me Eryn was missing, and I found her unconscious. I've never seen those jewels on her, either, but we both know she has no motive and—"

"The bank just refused her a massive loan." The sheriff crossed his arms over his chest. "Word in town is she's on the brink of bankruptcy and facing a divorce. I'll make sure we run the toxicology, but you might start getting used to the idea that your friend was desperate enough to do this." He stomped up the muddy hill, leaving Violet shaken and staring at the river.

Alex stepped forward and placed a hand on her back. "Hey. She's going to be okay. You and Teddy found her."

"Someone framed her." Her eyes searched his. "Why would someone do that? They drugged her like those two men did to you, except they clearly gave her a bigger dose."

"I don't know, but I'm going to find out." As he said the words, he racked his brain to figure out a possible motivation. He'd assumed they'd drugged him because the Firecracker or the mole on a target's security detail wanted to make sure he didn't have a flash drive. But why would they set up Eryn as a jewel thief?

Violet's shoulders sagged. "I want to catch the Firecracker, but I don't want everyone in my life to suffer because of that. Do you really think it's disconnected events?"

Alex didn't know what to say. He was certain Violet wasn't seeing things earlier. Someone had shone a laser scope in her office today, but they hadn't taken a shot. Why not? How did it all piece together? He missed his partner more than ever now, and his keen sense for solving puzzles. In fact, he wondered if Rick had died with the final clue to the Firecracker's identity. His very last words played on repeat in Alex's mind. *Something about this is starting to seem familiar.*

Violet's phone rang, and she answered with a lot of nodding before she hung up. "My law enforcement ranger team brought Callie, a German shepherd, out to help. She trailed the tracks behind the garage, but the scent ran cold at the highway."

Another dead end.

The last thing Violet wanted to do was get decked out for the second night in a row. The Waller Restaurant had a strict dress code, and the quick-change jacket Alex had worn the night before wasn't going to cut it. "The level of scrutiny is different than in the dark, in the woods. Besides that, your pants are all mussed up."

He shrugged, standing in the middle of her living room. "I'm wearing a different dress shirt, but beyond that, I don't have many choices packed with me."

She strode into the guest room and opened the closet where she kept a few of Rick's clothes. She told herself she'd brought them into the house for Teddy's sake, to have his scent nearby, but she'd also been known to sink her face into Rick's favorite sweaters during the first few months of mourning. It was probably time to let them go.

The charcoal suit, light blue shirt and silver tie caught her eye. She brushed her fingers over the fabric. It would fit Alex. The men had commented on being the same size when they wore the same exact thing as a joke to a charity dinner. She smiled at the memory, even though at the time, she had been so embarrassed to be seen with them.

Hanger in hand, she moved to leave and froze at the threshold. She'd been avoiding thinking or reflecting on her time with Rick for so long, in the hopes of avoiding the waves of pain. And yet she couldn't escape those thoughts with Alex around. She blew out a long breath. It was getting easier to think of Rick, easier to enjoy those memories. What an unexpected blessing to a horrible week.

A week that she hoped would end with catching Rick's killer.

She strode out into the hallway, where she found Alex had taken off his tuxedo tie, loosened it as far as it could go and was trying to put it around a waiting Teddy. Even with the added length, it didn't fit. "Well, can't say I didn't try to help him get with the dress code. Guess he can't come to dinner with us."

She laughed. "Dress code or not, Teddy goes where I go. I'm on call at all hours, but Daniella is scheduled to work the valet parking tonight."

"Daniella? Daniella who was volunteering at the district office? Wasn't she also working the party?"

"Yes. Her dad is in charge of the VIP clientele at the resort. She's taking on as much work as she can this year to save up for college. It's a gap year of sorts for her. She's almost twenty and working hard to get her life on track."

His attention moved to the suit in her

hands, and his eyes twinkled with held-back laughter. He held out his hands to accept the clothes. "Good choice. I'm sure Rick would approve." He disappeared to change in the bathroom, and her heart pounded from the words.

Teddy picked up the dropped tuxedo tie and whipped it around like a toy rope.

"Ah, man. That was a rental," Alex said from the hallway. He stepped fully into the light. There was nothing about him that looked like Rick. They may have worn the same-size suit, but their builds were completely different. Where Rick had been athletic in a track-and-field sort of way, Alex was built more like a wrestler. And yet he was wearing Rick's suit. He tilted his head and studied her reaction. "Violet? Are you sure? I can change if—"

"I'm fine," she said past the tightness in her throat. "I'd like to pull out the photo of the two of you from that night, and I can't." She gestured at the empty armoire.

"We'll figure out who took them and get the photos back. We can even postpone if—"

"No. Catching the Firecracker has to be the priority, Alex. It has to be."

He studied her face for a moment before turning. "Let's go, then." They got in the SUV so Teddy could ride in style. Violet started the vehicle, trying to mentally prepare herself to pretend to be on a date.

He pulled his seat belt on and faced forward. "I hate to do this, but…"

"You want to know how much I know about the Firecracker."

"Yes."

She knew the conversation was overdue. It was only natural. If she'd been the one investigating, she'd have tons of questions. "I didn't know you and Rick were working on a case involving the Firecracker until after his death."

"You never talked about it?"

She turned to face him briefly. "You know Rick played by the rules. He might mention what type of case he was working or if something was bothering him, but the details weren't fodder for dinner conversation. At least, not until the case was wrapped up. The last thing he told me about the one he was working was that something about it was starting to seem familiar."

"He said that to you?" Alex's voice rose in volume. "Did he say anything else?"

She startled and felt her eyes widen at his reaction. "That was it. Why?"

"He said the same thing to me..." Alex paled, obvious to her even in the dark vehicle. "But we didn't have a chance to discuss what he meant."

"We actually studied the Firecracker in college, so maybe that's why he said it seemed familiar."

"Really?" His question was full of hope.

"That criminal-profiling group I told you about? The Firecracker was a most-wanted fugitive even back then. He was one we picked to study as a deep-dive analysis. We discussed how we would track him down. What potential mistakes he could make? That sort of thing."

"Did you find any answers?"

She shook her head. "Not that I recall. His age stuck in my mind. I'd guess by now he'd be in his midfifties. But he disappeared for like fifteen years. We thought he'd retired."

"That matches what we have in our dossier, as well," Alex said as she pulled into the valet-parking loop and waited their turn.

"Why do you think he came out of retirement?"

"We're not sure. Maybe because of the advancement in explosives. Or he ran out of money."

"How do you know it's not a copycat?"

He smiled. "Good question. We have his DNA from two decades ago and some from a more recent assassination with the same MO. Unfortunately, when we run it, we find nothing that leads to his true identity. We thought we'd narrowed down a group of relatives, but there was no living connection. Maybe he was adopted."

Her phone buzzed, mercifully ending the discussion on her husband's killer. She tapped the button on her steering wheel that synced with her phone. "District Ranger Sharp." If she didn't have time to see the caller ID before answering, she went with her official title.

"It's Sheriff Bartlett." A tinge of static came through the speakers.

"Is Eryn okay?"

"Received the toxicology report." He sighed. "You made the right call. She was injected with something called midazolam. I'm told it's most often used for anesthesia. Miss Lane had enough in her system to keep her knocked out for a good four hours."

"When was the robbery?" Alex asked.

The sharp intake of breath over the speakers indicated the sheriff hadn't realized Alex was on the call, as well. She could only imagine the sheriff's level of irritation. "Since it will be public knowledge soon enough, the time of the robbery was three hours before you and Ranger Sharp arrived at the scene."

"So she was framed." Violet didn't realize her shoulders had made their way to her ears until she relaxed them. Her friend wouldn't be spending the night in jail.

"It would appear that way. Know any reason why someone would want to do that? We're fingerprinting her vehicle now, but it appears to have been wiped clean."

"Eryn is liked by everyone in this town." Even back in high school, she was one of the rare personalities who never offended anyone.

"Other than her husband?" the sheriff asked.

She cringed, unable to imagine Darren as capable of being that diabolical. "I really think they're trying to work it out.

They just wanted some time living apart while they're in counseling."

"In my experience, a wife doesn't try to get a loan without her husband if they plan to work it out."

Alex turned and placed a hand on her shoulder as she processed the sheriff's words. What had Eryn not been telling her? They were best friends, but this was a huge revelation and added a whole other level of confusion to everything that had been happening.

She took a deep breath. "Has she been discharged, then?"

"They're keeping her overnight due to the bump on her head, out of an abundance of caution, but she has a good prognosis. Call me if you think of anything else."

"Thank you, Sheriff." She hung up just as it was their turn to pull forward.

"This is a big ask, especially considering the circumstances, but I need you to act normal." Alex searched her face as if looking for evidence she could continue with the plan. "Like you're on a date."

She exhaled. "Except that's not normal. I haven't been on a date in seven years. I don't think anyone will expect me to act normal."

He faced forward. "That can work to our advantage. We'll keep it simple. Maybe slightly more familiar than sharing a casual meal with a friend. No need to fake romantic thoughts."

The last words made the back of her neck tingle. She could never fall for Alex, but the challenge he'd issued to not think romantic thoughts had the same result as if he were to tell her not to think about an elephant. What if she were to hold his hand again or stare deeply into his eyes? The thoughts were awkward enough to make her mouth go dry. But the thought of a cute elephant helped her switch gears as Daniella approached her driver's door with a smile.

"You should've called me. I would've

come over and done your hair. No red dots the rest of the day, I hope?" She smiled. "It was just some reflection, right?"

Violet didn't want to cause Daniella any fear, but she also didn't want to lie. "No more red dots. There was some activity near the storage garage behind the office, though. We're still investigating. Keep it on the down low, though. Okay? And don't report in for any volunteer shifts until we have more answers."

Daniella blinked, wide-eyed. "Wow. Okay. Hope your investigation turns out to be a curious raccoon. Does Teddy get to keep me company again?"

"Absolutely." She opened the back door, and Teddy made his way to the spot in front of the see-through fireplace that provided heat for whoever was working the valet booth.

Alex laughed. "He's done this before."

Daniella took the keys from Violet. "He's practically a tourist attraction. I've seen him mentioned in Yelp reviews, but

I think that's from the snowmobile safety demonstrations. He likes to ham it up when he's supposed to keep Violet from riding without a helmet."

"I'd love to see that." Alex reached for Violet's hand as Daniella drove away.

Violet took a deep breath and accepted his hand. Nothing romantic here. Just friends holding hands. Except her heart rate didn't believe it. They checked their coats and took the elevator up to the VIP-only floor.

"Just act comfortable and focus on the food. I'll be keeping an eye out for who is here, specifically trying to identify the security detail. If we pinpoint the target and the mole, then we can drop the cover and move in with backup."

"Understood."

"Thanks for helping out, Violet. I really appreciate it." He dropped her hand and briefly admired her curled hair and dress. The focused attention made her insides jittery. "We make a fine-looking pair."

She snorted, and the tension evaporated. Leave it to Alex to make a compliment that included himself. It was exactly the sort of story Eryn would find humorous. They used to share the funniest tales about their dates, and then later, about their husbands. It'd been years since they'd regaled each other with stories, though.

"Are you okay?" He slipped on his fake black-framed glasses.

"I'd like to visit with Eryn before the night is over, but yeah, I'm okay." The elevators slid open. "I can't rid myself of the feeling that Eryn's attack has something to do with me."

"I don't see how that's possible, but maybe once we find out who paid for your tickets last night, we can find out."

She'd forgotten about the tickets. He was right. She needed answers, and she felt certain Tom would be here tonight. Men in black suits, which no doubt hid weapons and earpieces, stood at opposite sides of the restaurant entrance. This time, as Alex reached for her fingers, she was ready.

SIX

Alex scanned his surroundings. The restaurant had no website—it was that exclusive—so this was the first chance he'd had to scope out potential exits. It was located on the top floor of the hotel, with a sharply sloped glass roof above him, and the stars twinkled like he'd never seen before. To the right, a man played soft jazz melodies on the piano.

The hostess beamed at Violet. "Tom was so excited you finally took him up on the standing reservation." She turned to Alex. "Welcome to the Waller Restaurant. Follow me."

Inside, the lighting glowed exclusively from candles. The diners sat at tables within recessed slots throughout the room. Outside, ski goggles and winter gear could hide identities. The restaurant kept the guests' desire for privacy in mind, and the place had been designed to help the rich and famous keep their anonymity. This made Alex's job more difficult. Roughly half a dozen men and two women in suits stood in the corners of the room, scanning the area.

"Are you wearing spy glasses?" Violet whispered. "I know Rick never had any, but a couple years have passed and technology…"

If only. He slowed his steps, and Violet followed. Alex placed a hand on her back and leaned over to whisper into her ear, an excuse so he could study the diners at the tables on the left. "Not even facial-recognition glasses, unfortunately. Can you pretend we stopped here like this because I had to tell you something sweet?" As he whispered, he spotted the governor at the next table and an actor that did action films, if he remembered right. He didn't recognize the other diners.

He straightened, and she flashed a flirtatious smile that caught him off guard, despite knowing he'd asked her to do so. Her presence so close to his side heightened his senses. Her hair smelled like strawberries and coconut. They caught up to the hostess, who sat them at the farthest inward table on the right, presumably closest to the kitchen, judging by the sounds.

Designed for intimate conversation, the table was only two feet deep and a good six feet from the other dining alcoves. It was easy enough to lean over and chat with your party without fear of being overheard. Speakers in between the tables softly broadcasted the piano music. Everything seemed to have been designed with discretion in mind. As the hostess left them with a list of specials, Violet leaned forward. "Did you notice anyone?"

"Only on the left side. The governor is dining here." He picked up the menu. No prices, of course. "I wasn't able to get a good look at the people on the right. I'll need to find another excuse to pointedly look that direction."

"It hit me that you hardly ever hear about assassination attempts in the news. Are they really that rare?"

"If we do our job well, they're stopped before ever getting a chance to be head-lined as an attempt. The Bureau doesn't typically seek publicity for what we do."

"Good point. Don't want to broadcast your methods too much, right?" The music switched to a slow ballad. Violet eyed the floor they'd just crossed. "If you're any good at a waltz, we can cover the entire floor."

He fought a grimace but stood. Violet was right that the dance floor would be the most natural place to stare at others without causing suspicion. If it'd been anyone else, if they'd been on a real date, he'd have declined. Hand-eye coordination came easy until he was asked to move to music.

He offered his hand, which she quickly accepted. As they stepped out onto the floor with four other couples, he kept a good twelve inches between them, with one hand lightly on her waist and the other holding her hand. The only thing he knew to do was get situated in a way he could see the tables on the right.

"Would you like me to lead?"

He shifted his attention to find an amused grin on her face.

"Alex, I don't think people consider standing in place to be the same thing as dancing."

"I guess now is the time to admit I've never waltzed." The piano melody transitioned into what was clearly an arrangement of a classic power ballad by Journey.

"That's good, because no one can waltz to this. Just step side to side and smile. We'll be fine. See anyone of note yet?"

There were no familiar faces at the first two tables. He'd studied multiple lists of potential high-value targets before this assignment. So far, no one matched. "Not yet. I need us to carefully make our way closer to the alcoves with the most guards."

"Okay. Here we go." She pressed against his hand, and they spun around and smoothly went back into casual, side-to-side swaying.

A laugh escaped him, despite the severity of the mission. "Thanks for leading."

"Don't mention it. I love this song."

His eyes dropped to hers for the briefest of seconds. In the middle of the turn, they'd somehow closed some distance between them and were now only six inches apart. "It's not country music."

Her smile broadened, and his breath caught for the slightest of moments. "You and Rick with your country music. No, thank you."

"Too bad. I guess I know how this

fake relationship is going to end. I could never be with someone who hates country music."

She nodded. "And I could never be with someone who doesn't like classic rock." The main line of the catchy chorus may not have been about faith, but he couldn't stop his mind from going there anyway. Violet and Rick had been very vocal about their faith. Alex didn't speak much about his, but he was a believer. "Do you still believe?"

She sighed, as if she'd anticipated the question. "Yes. But it doesn't mean that I don't have a heap of questions for my Maker when it's time."

"Same." He truly understood, and he was back to thinking about Rick's death. "Like why—?"

"Exactly." The decisive nod of her head meant she was done talking about that subject. "See anyone? Do we need to spin again?"

Right. Back to work. He studied the tables. "No one is jumping out."

"How do you know? Did you memorize a book of world leaders?"

He shrugged, not willing to admit to her that's basically what he'd done, only he'd studied a computer screen instead of a book. "Don't like to broadcast our methods, remember?"

"Hang on, then." She twisted her waist and pressed against his hand. A moment later, they'd spun across the floor. Alex fought to keep his shoulders from shaking with laughter. "The goal is to blend in, Violet, not draw everyone's attention."

She openly laughed along with him, and their eyes met. A connection like he'd never before experienced with her stole his breath away. She stiffened in his arms and worried her lip. She must have seen something. His gaze flew to the corners of the room. "What? What is it?"

"Uh...not sure. Nothing."

"You have a great instinct for undercover work, Violet. Never disregard anything that doesn't sit right."

"No, it's really nothing… I think I just have low blood sugar or something. Can we sit down? Have you seen enough?"

He had taken a good look around, and much to his disappointment, he didn't recognize anyone in the room except the governor. "Yeah. Let's order. Maybe we can stay until closing, in case someone else shows up."

She stepped out of his hands, and he followed her to their table. "It's slow food," she said once she was seated. "Meaning each table has only one party of guests reserved for each night. Dinner is supposed to take hours. What you see is what you get as far as the diners. The only exceptions come from being on the waiting list in case there's a cancellation." Alex's gaze drifted up to the mirror lining the top of the back wall. It was likely there to help the waiters keep an eye on the whole room at once, but Alex had a pretty good view of the people waiting to speak to the hostess from this vantage point.

A man in a navy suit, sporting a trim beard and the type of self-assured smile that could either belong in high-powered boardrooms or movies approached their table. Violet moved to stand, but the man waved her down. He leaned over and gave her a quick one-armed squeeze around her shoulders.

Alex forced a smile, surprised by the sour feeling in his stomach. Had Rick fought displeasure at seeing Alex give Violet a friendly hug whenever he came over? He doubted it, though there was one major difference. Rick had been 100 percent confident in Violet's love for only him. Besides, Alex had never had a single thought for Violet other than friendship. So what was wrong with him this week?

He was watching out for her safety, and any man intruding in her personal space was a threat. Yes, that was it.

The man turned to him and offered a

right hand. A firm, honest handshake. "You must be Alex. I'm Tom, Daniella's dad. Whatever you said to convince Violet to come to dinner here, thank you. I always keep one table open to fill as I see fit. I've been trying to get Violet to come for ages."

A soft rosy glow he'd rarely seen crossed Violet's features. For a brief moment, she wasn't a US Forest Ranger, his partner's widow or even a friend. She was a woman with beautiful hazel eyes out on a date. He'd never noticed her eyes before. Dazzling. The change in his perception caught him off guard. She really could do undercover work well. That was all.

"I told you it wasn't necessary, Tom," she said.

"Let me thank you in the only way I know how." Tom turned back to Alex. "Violet changed the trajectory of Daniella's life. Probably saved her life, if I'm being honest. Her mother and I can't even tell you." His eyes glistened briefly.

"He's exaggerating."

Tom straightened and placed a hand on his heart. "I am not."

Violet fidgeted with her cloth napkin. "I only mentored her, and by God's grace, she responded. Our personalities just suit each other. I love Daniella. It's my pleasure to spend time with her."

"Whatever the reason, please enjoy dinner tonight. Enjoy yourself for once. On the house." He turned to Alex, and in an instant, the man's face transformed into an expression usually reserved for enemies. "Be sure you treat our Violet right. She works tirelessly for this community, and we want only the best for her." As fast as the dangerous narrowing of eyes appeared, all animosity vanished and he smiled again at Violet.

"Before you go—" Violet held up a finger and leaned toward Tom conspiratorially. "You organized the governor's dinner at the River Run, right?"

"I was the venue contact," he clarified.

"Were the locals invited to come, too? For free?"

His eyebrows jumped, and he laughed. "Not even for you, Violet. Sorry. The event was two thousand dollars a plate."

"I was actually there, though. Someone sent me an invitation. They must have bought my ticket and Eryn's. I'd like to find out who. Is it possible you could get access to that information?"

"I don't touch the ticket money, only the venue contract fees." His brow furrowed. "That sort of thing becomes public soon enough, though, since it was a political fundraiser. If it can't wait, I'd ask the treasurer handling the governor's reelection campaign."

"Oh? Is the treasurer here?"

"Not tonight, but he's a townie. Do you know Chris Sebatke?"

Her mouth dropped. "His older sister used to babysit me. Yes, I know Chris. I'll see if we can reconnect." She smiled. "Speaking of the governor, there's a lot of suits here. More bodyguards than I would imagine for your normal clientele. Is there a senator here, too, perhaps? Secret Service?"

When Alex thought he couldn't respect Violet any more, she surprised him. Smooth.

Tom leaned over and pointed at the menu, as if discussing the specials. "Federal Reserve Police," he said quietly. "Between me and you, they're more cautious than the troopers and Secret Service we've worked with in the past."

Alex's heart went into overdrive. "The Federal Reserve chair?"

Tom's gaze flickered over to him, surprise that Alex had joined the conversation written on his face. He addressed Violet when he answered. "Mark Leonard is on the board of governors but is rumored to be announced as a nominee for the chair next week." He straightened. "Enjoy your dinner."

The moment Tom disappeared around

the corner, Violet's eyes widened. Had they always been so vibrant? "That's the type of powerful position you were looking for, right?"

A federal nominee *would* be the type of target the Firecracker would come out of hiding for. There would be a high price on the man's head. This was the type of lead that could help the Bureau stop the assassination in its tracks. The rumored mole would likely be on the Federal Reserve Police detail. Alex would have to tread cautiously so as not to alert the mole, but he'd also need to make sure Mark Leonard stayed safe.

He'd never been this close to bringing down the Firecracker. The strange happenings of the week wouldn't leave him alone, though. The missing photographs, the red dot in the forest service office and the drugging of Violet's friend. He couldn't find a motive to connect them all, and as he took a bite of what was no doubt the best bread ever to meet his taste buds, he was unable to enjoy it. Because with everything going on, how could he trap the Firecracker while also keeping Violet safe?

This had to be the most uncomfortable meal she'd ever experienced with Alex. Pretending to be in a relationship had seemed easy enough, until they'd started laughing. A shared laugh had never felt so confusing before. She hadn't meant to be silly, but she also had never needed to lead a man in a dance before.

"Did you notice a woman with long black hair and a red dress at the governor's dinner?" His gaze stayed focused on something above her head. Odd.

"That's like asking me if I noticed a candle in the restaurant. There were a lot of women there. Can you be more specific?"

He shook his head and narrowed his eyes, his gaze still above her. She moved to look over her shoulder. "No, don't look at the mirror," he said. "I don't want to draw attention. See if you can casually look over my shoulder to spot who I'm talking about. She's wearing a black pantsuit and standing in line to talk to the hostess. Not black hair this time. She's blond now."

A waiter walked past them with a large tray of plates, blocking the view of the lobby. She strained but couldn't see past him. "Are you sure it's the same woman?"

"Not a hundred percent sure, but if I'm right, that's the Firecracker's courier." He groaned as the waiter returned to the kitchen. "She's gone."

"Maybe she went to the restroom. How about I go find out?"

He paled. "If it's the same woman, she might recognize you. After all, someone did find your purse and switch the flash drives."

The back of her neck tightened. "Which means the two men who tried to drug you could also be nearby." She slipped her hand into her purse. "I understand the danger, but I feel like you keep forgetting that I'm trained in law enforcement, too. I'm armed this time, Alex, as I assume you are. She could lead us to the Firecracker now, and we could end this. Let's get our coats and go find her."

"I don't think Rick—"

"Would want me in danger?" She slipped her purse strap over her shoulder. "I think we can both agree all the weird stuff happening this week might mean I'm in danger already. And let's get something straight. This resort is on land in partnership with the forest service. I am a ranger of the forest service, and even though I'm not currently deputized with the sheriff, like my law enforcement rangers, I still have authority to arrest anyone who breaks federal laws."

"Are you arguing jurisdiction?"

"No. I'm telling you that Rick knew I faced danger daily. It's time for you to accept that and maybe allow me to help." A flash of black behind the hostess podium caught her eye, and she stood. "I'm going to check the restroom to see if she went in there. Please let Tom know we're leaving. Maybe he'll be able to tell you the name that woman goes by if she's a regular. I'll meet you by the elevator."

She strode across the restaurant, lifted her coat off the rack with one hand and draped it over the arm where her purse dangled. The coat concealed the fact she was removing her weapon from her purse so she would be ready to fire, should she need to. The little speech she'd given Alex wasn't like her, really, but at least it had cast all thoughts of attraction to the far recesses of her mind. It was time to work.

Thankfully, the area in front of the restrooms was empty. There was no sign of the two men who had grabbed Alex the night before. She hadn't got a good look at their faces that night, but she remembered their builds. She kept the gun pointed at forty-five degrees, still hidden by the coat, and opened the door to the ladies' room with her foot. There were no sounds from inside, except instrumental music playing from the speaker in the ceiling. Moments later, she'd confirmed there was no one in the stalls.

She stepped outside to find a flustered Alex standing with his coat and a large brown bag.

"What's in the bag?"

"Tom insisted you couldn't leave without dessert. He might also want to murder me after I asked about the woman. I think he thought I was trying to pick up another date while out with you."

She fought against a smile, but her lips wouldn't stop twitching. "Nice to know I've got people watching my back."

"I think it's safe to say he disapproves of your first serious fake relationship." Alex looked around the corner. "I don't see the numbers on the elevator moving. Stairs?"

A quick look in his direction confirmed he held his weapon underneath his coat, as well. He followed her gaze. "Do they train rangers to cover their guns like that?"

"No, but FBI special agents married to rangers sometimes enjoy procedural discussions. We picked up tips from one another." They worked in tandem, both angling the opposite direction every time they reached a landing and peeking out at the hallways. Violet tried not to linger on how natural partnering with Alex felt.

"Did you ever help Rick with one of our cases?"

"Like I said, we didn't usually talk about work, but you remember that arson case?"

His mouth dropped. "Rick told me he just happened to know a lot about trees. It was you, wasn't it?"

She shrugged, knowing Rick would've gotten a kick out of seeing the shocked look on Alex's face. "Maybe."

They reached the bottom lobby, and she noticed Alex's shoulders sagged.

"I think it's safe to say we lost her," he said.

"Is it time to shed the undercover role and check the security cameras of the resort?"

He cringed. "Maybe. Though that will no doubt get back to the suits of the Federal Reserve Police. I was hoping to avoid that."

She nodded. "Then maybe I put a call into Stephen. He's Daniella's boyfriend. He works in the security office. I might be able to casually tell him to look out for the woman and two men. He's not the type to ask too many questions, especially since he knows I work for the forest service."

"Thank you. How about we head back then? I think it's time I have a long talk with my handler back at the Bureau. There might be enough here to bring in backup."

They reached the valet parking where Daniella was handing over keys to a couple. Teddy stretched from his spot in front of the fireplace and ambled over to her. "Long day, huh, buddy?"

"He was great, as usual," Daniella said over her shoulder. "Greeted some of the guests who wanted to say hi. Mostly, he napped."

Violet reached down to pet him, and the corner of some stiff paper scratched at her palm. She bent over. "What've you got there, boy?" She pulled the offending paper out from underneath his vest and flipped it over.

The photograph of Rick and Alex dressed in identical suits and goofy grins stared up at her. It was the photo from the charity event that she'd remembered earlier. The same red marker that had circled her face in the wedding photograph now circled Alex's face in this picture.

"Violet?" Alex's cupped her shoulders. "What is it?"

The hand that held the photo began shaking despite her attempts to remain calm. She straightened and held it out to him. He took one look, spun around and stepped in front of her, as if protecting her. Whoever was trying to torture her had gotten close to Teddy. Her heart went into overdrive. "Daniella, describe everyone who spent time with Teddy."

"I don't know." Daniella looked at her as if she'd grown an extra head. "The usual tourist types. Anyone who loves a dog." Her face scrunched up. "Someone gave him one of those big meat sticks he likes."

Alex jolted at the same time she did. "Who? Who gave Teddy something to eat?"

"I never saw who. Only saw he was enjoying one. I was too busy helping guests."

Violet held out her hand. "Throw me my keys."

Daniella's eyes widened, but she did as she asked. Violet patted the side of her leg, and Teddy ran alongside her. He was too big for her to carry, and she needed to get him seen right away.

Alex ran up alongside her. "Taking him to the vet? You're worried about poison?"

"Wouldn't you be?" They reached her vehicle and got Teddy inside.

He sighed and nodded. "Let's go."

She just hoped they could get him help in time.

SEVEN

Alex stared at the photo of himself and his partner in matching suits. It was hard to remember a time that he'd allowed himself to be goofy for the sake of a good laugh. He stuffed the picture back in his pocket, his mind swirling.

He'd yet to reveal his presence to the Federal Reserve Police, but given what had happened with Teddy, Alex requested access to the security footage. Now the Idaho state troopers who guarded the governor knew he was FBI. They had gotten back to him a moment ago to reveal the security tapes of the hallways and portico had been set to loop on footage from the previous night. Security had been breached.

Violet exited a swinging door and joined him in the lobby of the vet hospital. "Doc said he can induce vomiting instead of pumping Teddy's stomach." She let out a shaky breath. "They don't think he was poisoned. They're running a few more tests to make sure he looks good." She sank into the closest orange plastic chair and dropped her head into her hands. "I can't lose Teddy."

He sat next to her and placed a hand on her back. She wouldn't handle the news of the security footage well. If the cameras could be compromised despite state troopers and Federal Reserve Police working with hotel security, then how could they keep their protectees safe against the Firecracker?

"You won't lose Teddy," he said instead. "We're going to find whoever is doing this and put a stop to it."

She placed a hand on top of his. "Thanks, but you don't have to do that."

"Do what?"

"Promise justice. Because we work in law enforcement, it seems like something we can control, doesn't it? But if Rick's killer can get away—"

"We're going to get him, too, Violet." The words held no luster, though. She was right, yet again. Repeatedly saying he'd catch the killer wouldn't make his promise come true. "At least, I pray we'll catch him."

She gave him a soft smile. "I'll join you in that prayer. But while we wait, I'd like to talk about something else for now. If that's okay?"

He flipped his hand over to properly hold hers. His mind whirled with questions about the case, but for her sake, he strained to find a new subject, at least for a few minutes. "You enjoy mentoring Daniella?"

She casually dropped his hand and leaned back into the chair, wrapping the dress coat tighter around herself. "I don't know if it's the mentoring I enjoy or who

I'm hanging out with. I suppose in the back of my mind, I've realized it's the closest I'll get to motherhood."

He vividly remembered Rick discussing their dilemma about starting a family. It hadn't been a matter of if, but when. Rick had told him he'd request a desk position within the FBI once he became a father. Alex had struggled with that news as it meant he'd lose his partner. Now, after years in the field undercover, a desk-jockey position sounded like a dream come true. "You adore kids, if memory serves."

He used to think he'd want a family someday, but if he couldn't even protect the people in his life now, how could he possibly be a good father? Fathers protected their families. They died for them. Alex had sent the friend he considered a brother to his death because of a bad judgment call. Had he been making bad calls while he was with Violet, too?

"I adore the kids I know, at least." She

sighed. "Speaking of which, I need to check in with Eryn since we're so close to the hospital. She might like some help with her kids. I don't know what her current arrangement is with her husband."

The back door opened, and Teddy bounded through. Violet and Alex jumped to their feet and went to either side of the dog to pet him.

"I believe he's fine," the balding vet said. "We fed him a small second dinner, and he's doing great. If he shows any concerning signs, you have my number. Don't hesitate to call." The vet leaned down and petted the top of Teddy's head before disappearing into the back again.

Violet straightened. "Ready to go, boy?" She looked at Alex. "Do you mind if we stop at the hospital? Eryn would probably like a chance to thank her rescuer."

"They'll let Teddy in the hospital?"

"Official K-9s are allowed. Besides,

Teddy's kind of a celebrity there, as well. He's saved so many lives."

"As have you."

"I wouldn't have been able to without Teddy." They got inside the vehicle, and her phone vibrated. "Official call. One second."

Alex couldn't hear what was being said, but Violet's silence spoke volumes. Her eyes grew wider and her breath shallow. He was about to reach for the phone when she finally said, "Understood. Bring in all LEOs. This is top priority... Yes. Let me know as soon as you know." She hung up and paled.

"Violet?" He knew that LEOs meant she was calling in all law enforcement officers within her forest district. "What's going on?"

"Remember the garage behind my office?"

He held his breath. "What's happened?"

"Our snow ranger needs to confirm, but

one of my team thinks we might have some explosives missing."

"Bombs are missing?" He enunciated every word, and his head throbbed with the sudden increase in his blood pressure. That's all he needed. Trying to capture an assassin that specialized in blowing up people, and explosives were missing. At Violet's slight nod, he wanted to punch something. "And they just now discovered this?"

"After the mysterious red dot incident, the rangers were cataloging the storage in the garage. We keep the explosives in a special safe. There was no sign of tampering, so they didn't check the contents first. They're bringing in my lead snow ranger for avalanche control to confirm their suspicions. It's not a simple job. We need him to look over his logs to rule out human error. There are checks and balances. If the log sheet doesn't match the contents of the safe but does match the recent avalanche-mitigation efforts, then problem solved. It's unlikely, but everyone makes mistakes."

"If there are bombs missing, then game over. We fill the hotel with bomb-sniffing K-9s." They'd also lose their chance to catch the Firecracker, but Violet didn't need to be told the obvious.

"I know how serious this is, but I also don't want to create a false panic."

"What kind of explosives? What's the magnitude?"

"The snow rangers use a variety of types based on the conditions and the location. Different needs, different kinds. We have small snow shots. Those need to be manually detonated from a distance."

"How powerful are we talking?"

"You step on one wrong, and it takes off your foot. We use half a dozen at a time, usually. But we also have a fairly new system of remote-detonated explosives. We place those in the harder-to-access mountains. We can set those off no matter the weather or time, so we can limit highway closures."

He groaned. "I'm guessing those are more powerful?"

"Yes. But harder to take and walk away with."

"Except we saw tracks."

"Yes. I'm aware. They're going to call me back as soon as the snow ranger arrives."

"How much does the log say is missing?"

"Enough to set off a few avalanches."

He closed his eyes for a second to ease the pain building in his temples. "I need to let the troopers know—"

"They know." She turned to him. "My snow ranger notified the police and the troopers before he called me, out of an abundance of caution."

"Please tell me the moment you have confirmation." He needed to phone his supervisor to discuss how to proceed. Even if he was called off the case, he was staying until he could figure out who was tormenting Violet and those she cared about. "You're not going to like it, but—"

"You also want to ask Eryn questions."

He huffed. "That's unnerving, you know."

"Sorry. It's what I would do in your situation. You're trying to figure out the connection and why someone is targeting me and the people closest to me." Her voice shook ever so slightly. "It'll mean breaking your cover, though. Eryn won't believe a boyfriend in the hospitality industry would be asking such questions."

"I'm aware." With the news about missing bombs, staying undercover seemed like the least of his concerns.

She took the first right turn as the hospital parking lot was adjacent to the animal hospital. They parked in the visitors' section and made quick work of getting to the second floor before visiting hours ended.

Eryn Lane, a petite woman with short

blond hair, looked small in the hospital bed. She blinked, bleary-eyed, and turned her focus from the television to the doorway. "Violet!" She reached her hands out. Violet and Teddy hustled to her bedside. Teddy waited patiently for their hug to be done and then lightly pressed his paws on the edge of the bed and lifted his head for Eryn to show her appreciation. "My hero."

"How are you?" Violet asked.

"I'm perfectly fine now. They're just taking precautions. I can't thank you enough for proving my innocence."

"I'm sorry you're in this situation. I have a feeling it has something to do with me."

Eryn flinched. "How could that be?"

Violet looked over her shoulder at Alex. His cue. "Eryn, I'm actually FBI special agent Alex Driscoll. I'm here on a separate investigation, but someone seems to be intent on targeting those closest to Violet this week. Can I ask you a few questions?"

"Of course." Her mouth dropped open and her eyes slid to Violet. "You're not really dating?"

"Afraid not. He needed to stay undercover, and that was the easiest ruse we could come up with."

"That's a relief. No offense." Eryn gestured toward him. "I was pretty miffed you'd kept something like that from me."

"I think you've been keeping a few things from me, as well," Violet said gently.

Eryn flushed, and Alex could tell they needed to talk. "Let me get a few questions out of the way, and then I'll give you some privacy. Did you pay for the ticket to the governor's dinner?"

"Pay?" Eryn scrunched up her nose. "It was free. I was invited, but I had to RSVP."

"To who?"

Eryn looked up. "There was a phone number on the invite."

Violet blinked. "Mine didn't have a phone number."

"I had to give my name and a few demographic-type details for their stats or something."

Violet's intrigued reaction likely matched his own. There was a lot of information that could be gathered from a demographic survey. "Violet, you didn't RSVP to anyone?"

She shook her head. "No, I went as Eryn's plus one."

"They had her info, though," Eryn said. "I gave it to them since she was my guest."

"I'll need to get that number from you. Last question. Can you think of anyone in town, anyone from high school or your shared past who would have a grudge against you both?"

Eryn frowned. "Are you serious? Is he serious? We were like the two most goody-two-shoes girls in school. Nice to everyone."

Alex turned to Violet. "That seems hard to imagine."

"Growing up in a small town, you don't really have the option to make many enemies. It wouldn't be wise, at least. We weren't exactly doormats, though."

"Anything but," Eryn added.

"Okay. That's all for now." Alex gestured to the hallway. "I need to make a phone call. Mind if I do so in your SUV? I can pull it around to pick you up."

"Sure." Violet handed him the keys. "Teddy and I will join you in a few minutes."

He strolled back through the hospital, deep in thought. If it weren't for the men who'd tried to drug him as well as Eryn, he'd dismiss any potential connection between the Firecracker and the actions taken against Violet.

The photo in his pocket meant that

someone knew he was close to Rick. Could this all be about Rick or Violet?

That would make sense only if he was missing something about his former partner's murder. To bring it up again, in detail, was something he'd never wanted to do with Violet, and yet he knew he'd never have peace until he did. She was the one person who might fill in the missing pieces from that day. But if she learned the whole truth about Rick's death, would she ever be able to look him in the eye again?

"You're really okay? Didn't hit your head too hard?" Violet asked, hating the thought of what those men could've done to Eryn.

"Physically, I'm almost one hundred percent. They ran tests and checked me out, and I'm fine. For that, I'm very relieved. The worst part was not knowing how I got there and seeing that jewelry on and around me." Eryn's eyes watered.

"There was the smallest part of me that wondered if I was losing my mind."

Violet reached for her friend's hand and held it. Teddy made a noise in his throat that sounded like his attempt at soothing sounds before he flopped down on the ground at her feet. He'd had a rough day, as well, and all because of her. If only she understood who would do such a thing and why.

"What the sheriff said about loans and bankruptcy...are you in some kind of trouble?"

Eryn shook her head and closed her eyes. "No. When I agreed to try separation, Darren talked about selling the house and splitting the proceeds. I don't want to take the kids from the only home they've ever known, so I tried to get a loan for his half of the house to pay him outright."

Her mouth dropped open. "That's so much to take on yourself." Her throat tightened at the realization of the burden Eryn had been carrying alone. Alex had been right. People saw what they wanted to see. And she'd wanted to see her friends without real hurts and struggles. A groan built in her throat. "I thought you guys were in counseling. I had no idea. Why didn't you tell me any of this?"

Eryn turned away, a faint blush on her cheeks. "You had your own stuff to deal with."

When Violet first returned to Sunshine Valley, she'd been newly widowed. She'd practically had a sign on her forehead that read I Can't Handle Any Big Emotions. Not that she didn't care, but she hadn't been able to share anyone's burdens or even their joys. But now?

With sinking dread, she realized she'd made it clear to anyone who knew her that finding love and happiness again wasn't possible for her. Hadn't she said as much to Alex the other night? Who would be comfortable sharing highs and lows with a friend who'd declared that? No wonder they'd been trying so hard to play matchmaker.

"I'm so sorry I've been pushing away any real conversations about the tough stuff." Violet squeezed Eryn's hand. "I want to be here for you the way you've been for me."

Eryn let her head sink back into the pillow with a sigh. "I'd like that. And as far as Darren goes... I think we might have a chance again after all." She gestured at the hospital gown. "This gave him a scare. Not that I'd ever advise getting drugged and left for dead as a treatment for struggling marriages."

Violet pulled her chin back. She'd never imagined anything good could come out of something so horrible.

"Time will tell, I suppose," Eryn said. "Enough about me. *That* was Rick's partner?" Her eyes narrowed, and her eyebrows jumped. "It's more than a cover, isn't it? There's something there." Eryn gasped. "Oh, I see it on your face. There is."

Violet's neck felt like it was on fire. Teddy shifted and pressed against her legs, confirming that her emotions were running hot. "I... I don't know. And even if there were, it would never work."

Eryn crossed her arms. "Why not?"

Violet faltered, surprised by the intensity of the question and how it stumped her. The answer had seemed easy a week ago when all relationships had been off the table. When Rick died, she'd thought she would literally perish from the pain of losing him. Each day that she woke up was a surprise to find that her own heart was still beating and her lungs still breathing without him there.

She'd eventually resumed eating and drinking—albeit less—mostly thanks to her stubborn mom. Grief physically hurt. Her entire body ached all the time. The only thing that had helped her was movement. At first, it was to take care of Teddy, because he relied on her. She'd needed to keep up his training for his sake.

Teddy was miserable without his work, and she knew he missed Rick, too. She could see it in his eyes and the way he held his head. And she'd realized if she kept moving, the pain didn't hurt as much. She couldn't think or feel with as much intensity if she stayed active, working on a problem that was right in front of her.

"The first year was hard, and the second year was harder somehow," she finally told Eryn. "I don't know why it was harder, but I just tried to stop feeling. I don't know when it started getting easier. Sometimes it's a shock to realize I'm not in pain, and other times it hits me like a bolt of lightning out of nowhere, and I fall apart all over again."

"But you seem like yourself again with Alex. I saw it myself."

Her heart jolted with the realization

Eryn was right. She had felt like herself with him many times. "He mentions Rick," she finally said. "I didn't know that I craved someone else talking about him. Alex gets how important it is to keep his memory alive, maybe because he misses him almost as much as I do." She exhaled slowly. "He's not holding his breath or looking at me like I'm going to break down if he says Rick's name. It's nice."

"I'm very glad." Eryn shook her head slowly. "But I'm telling you that's not all it is."

Her stomach flipped. "Maybe it's just about finding out who killed Rick and who is putting my friends and Teddy in danger."

"No. I've known you since fifth grade, and while you've changed a lot, one thing remains the same."

Eryn's calm refusal was beginning to infuriate her, and she placed her hands on her hips. "Oh, yeah? And what's that?"

"Whenever you like a boy, you bite

your lip. You do it whenever you think about Alex or look at him." Eryn's eyes twinkled.

Violet didn't think her mouth and eyes had ever grown so wide. "I..." A breath of air that sounded somewhere between a laugh and a gasp escaped. "I do not!"

"You do. You *so* do." Eryn wiped the tears from laughing away. "It's cute. You did it with Leo in junior high, Bruce in high school and the first time you brought Rick home to meet your parents." Teddy lifted his head, watching their interchange carefully. "See, even Teddy agrees with me," Eryn added.

"Don't bring Teddy into this." She found herself laughing while tears escaped out the corners of her eyes. Even amid the frustrating mysteries and danger surrounding her, she'd laughed more this week than in the past two years. The thought sobered her.

"What? What is it?"

"Is it weird that I'm scared to feel...?"

She couldn't fully voice what was swirling in her heart and mind.

Eryn reached for her. "Violet, you're not forgetting Rick. And having a laugh or even feelings for another guy doesn't diminish the love you had for him..." Violet's breath caught, and Eryn quickly added, "...will always have for him."

Her shoulders dropped, even her limbs felt lighter. "Hey, you're the one in the hospital. You're not supposed to be helping me."

"I've never experienced loss like you have, but I watched you go through it with your dad. Remember years ago, that summer during college, when you were at my house and that song came on?"

She instantly remembered. It was the song she and her dad always used to dance to. When he'd first passed away, she couldn't hear it without breaking down. But years later at Eryn's house, she'd found herself wanting to dance to it instead of crying.

"You said you could enjoy the memory again. Doing that dance helped you feel closer to that memory."

"I remember." Yet this felt different. She didn't have the words to explain, so she simply offered a smile.

"Eryn?" Darren stood in the doorway with a giant bouquet of flowers. "Is this a bad time?"

Eryn's eyes softened at the sight of him, and she glanced at Violet for a second, as if asking for permission. Violet leaned over and hugged her friend. "No more holding out on me. Both the good and the bad. Okay?" she whispered. "I can take it now."

Eryn's brows rose. "Are you sure?"

"I'm sure. Though no more matchmaking and leave the body-language profiling to the professionals. Maybe my lip was just chapped." Violet winked at Eryn and offered a small wave to Darren as Teddy joined her in the hallway.

She strolled out of the hospital, still reflecting on their discussion. There was a lot of processing to do over the events of the night and the conversation with Eryn. An early bedtime would help her do that. Biting her lip when she liked a guy? As if.

Snow began to fall in fat flakes and hit the tip of her nose. There was no sign of Alex and her SUV. She'd thought he was going to pull up to the entrance or at least be watching for her. His call might've gone longer than expected, or maybe he'd gotten distracted. Good thing she'd slipped into the boots she kept in the vehicle when they'd gone to the vet, or the cold gust of air would've been an unwelcome surprise. She patted her leg, and they rounded the corner, past the streetlight to where she'd parked.

Two figures in the distance caught her attention. Teddy grumbled, and she felt him stiffen beside her. Two men fighting. She squinted. Was that Alex?

Teddy barked, sending shivers up her

spine. An arm snaked around her neck. She'd been so focused on the pair of men, she'd missed someone sneaking up behind her!

Hot breath hit her ear. "Someone wants to have a word with you."

A fist lifted, and out of the corner of her eye, she spotted the syringe. She shoved her elbow into the man's side. He barely moved but the interchange stalled him from shoving the needle in her shoulder. She felt Teddy shift behind him.

"Off!" the man shouted.

She stomped her feet and slammed her heel onto his instep. He yelped, and the moment his grip loosened, she stepped forward. Teddy rose up on his hind legs and jumped onto the man's chest, shoving him backward. The man stumbled, turned and ran away just as a gunshot rang out behind her. She spun around. "Alex."

Teddy didn't hesitate. He ran toward the two figures. One of them broke away and also raced off. She sprinted in their direction to find Alex hunched over, and Teddy sniffed him wildly, as if checking him over for injuries. "Are you okay?"

His weary eyes met hers. "More importantly, are you?"

"I think so. He got the jump on me and tried to drug me." She whirled around. "I think he might've dropped the syringe. But I heard a gunshot?"

"My gun. I reached my weapon but when he tried to wrestle it out of my hands, I fired a warning shot into the air. It spooked him enough that he let go and ran." Alex turned on his phone flashlight and walked with her back toward the corner where the syringe would be. The plastic reflected off the beam. "Maybe we can get some prints off this. I don't suppose you have an evidence bag or gloves handy for me to pick it up?"

"I might, in the vehicle." Her voice wobbled, taking her by surprise. She'd spent so long building up a protective layer to keep from feeling too much, and this week was breaking it apart bit by bit.

He reached for her instead of the syringe and pulled her closer. "Are you sure you're okay?"

"I think so."

He looked down, searching her face. "Violet, don't hide your pain from me. You're clearly biting your lip."

Heat flooded her stomach, and she closed her eyes. She hated that Eryn knew her so well. Was she truly attracted to Alex? "It's just a lot to process," she whispered.

He responded by wrapping his arms tightly around her. Her cheek rested against his chest, underneath his chin, and for a moment, all she could hear was the beating of his heart. They stood there quietly, until a bright beam of light hit her squarely in the face.

The sheriff stepped out of his vehicle, pointing his flashlight, as well, at them. "What's going on here?"

EIGHT

The first thing Alex noticed was the sheriff's hand on his weapon as he stood with his door still open. It was a tactical move in case he needed protection. Why would the sheriff think he needed to protect himself against them?

"I was looking for you, Violet. Word around town is you went to the animal hospital and then to see Eryn." The sheriff raised his voice over a gust of wind that carried a burst of stinging snow. As he spoke, two other patrol cars sped toward the parking lot with their lights flashing but sirens off. "En route, I heard about a gunshot behind the hospital. Something you need to tell me?" His eyes remained trained on Alex's side, where his coat had slipped up, exposing his gun.

Violet spun out of his embrace. "I can explain."

Alex stepped in front of Violet, holding has hands up to the sheriff. "I think it's time to properly introduce myself. FBI special agent Alex Driscoll. Two men, the men I suspect are behind Eryn's drugging and likely the jewelry store robbery, attacked us minutes ago. I fired my weapon but didn't hit anyone."

"FBI, huh?"

"I was actually about to call you," Violet added. She turned and pointed at the ground. "They tried to drug me. I'm hoping you can find prints on the syringe."

The two deputy vehicles pulled up in formation behind the sheriff. He held up a hand to indicate they should wait. "Before we continue, I'd like to see your badge, Mr. Driscoll. Nice and slowly, if you please."

Alex complied. Thankfully, he had it on

his person today. He'd brought it along in case he needed to discuss intel with the troopers. He reached in his coat with his right hand and produced the badge.

The sheriff reached for his radio. "Stand down. Return to your posts." He stomped through the rapidly building snow and took the badge from Alex. The flashlight beam illuminated the unflattering photo from back when Alex thought a buzz cut suited him. Rick and Violet had been the ones to encourage him to let his thick, wavy hair grow a bit. They'd said it made him look more mature, which had appealed to him at the time.

"You're dating an FBI agent, Vi?" the sheriff asked. Alex had never heard someone call her by that nickname.

Her spine stiffened. Clearly, she wasn't a fan. "It was a cover to help him find Rick's killer, Sheriff."

The man's eyes widened, and he looked between them both. "Did you?"

"Still hoping," Alex said. "We don't

know if these unusual happenings are connected."

"The man who tried to drug me said that someone wanted to talk to me." She shook her hands in front of her as if trying to shake something off her person.

"What?"

"The adrenaline and the gunshot... For a second, I thought you'd been hit." Her voice trembled, but she steeled her features. "I'm still going over the details in my mind. But yes, I'm sure my attacker said something to that effect." She squatted, staring at the syringe in the snow. "You have gloves?"

The sheriff removed some from his harness and gingerly picked up the syringe. "This relates to why I came to find you." He slipped the item carefully into a thick bag and stood. "We had another robbery. This time the art gallery. Over a million dollars' worth of art and statues were stolen."

Alex whistled. "I'm surprised a small

town has a gallery showcasing items of that kind of worth." In his experience, the art found in small towns usually graced the walls of local cafes and coffee shops, with price tags underneath them.

"This is not a normal small town," she explained. "Our tourists can afford it and often want to buy something while on vacation. It's why we have such a famous jewelry store, as well." Violet turned to the sheriff. "That's not why you came to find me. If you needed the forest service, you'd call my law enforcement rangers. You need Teddy?"

He nodded. "Bruce Wilkinson is missing. His vehicle was found near the gallery."

She released an exasperated sigh. "Don't tell me he's a suspect."

"I follow the evidence." The sheriff gestured at the hospital. "But if this is like Eryn's experience, it might be in Bruce's interest to be found sooner rather than later." He raised his chin into the flurries. "Snow and temps dropping fast. You know I can't call the search-and-rescue team in so quickly and without more information. But since you and Bruce had a relationship—"

"In high school," she said, her annoyance shining through.

"Pretty easy to follow your love life when you've only had one boyfriend and one husband." His eyes darted to Alex. "And one fake boyfriend."

"Why'd I think it was a good idea to move back to my hometown?" Violet muttered under her breath. "Fine."

"I don't think assigning this to Violet is the right call." Alex addressed the sheriff. "Someone is targeting her. They tried to get me out of the picture, and they want to kidnap her. She's in danger, and I don't—"

"That's not your decision to make, Agent Driscoll," Violet said. "I'm used to being in danger as part of my job, and I said I'd do it. Someone is targeting everyone I know, which makes me responsible, and I'd like to catch whoever is behind this more than anyone. Teddy has had a rough night, though." She turned back to the sheriff. "If we don't find Bruce within a few hours, you'll need to call in some officers to take over. Can't you justify it since technically Bruce is a suspect in the robbery?"

The sheriff's lips twisted to one side. "I'd prefer not to do that when I don't think he's guilty, but I'm willing. You know I can't page for a SAR team so soon in this instance. It doesn't fit the guidelines."

"I know." Violet blew out a long breath, and Teddy scooted closer to her.

"Please keep us updated on what you find out." Alex pointed to the evidence bag.

"Will do. Stay safe." The sheriff backed up and took the same route out of the lot as the other deputies. Violet watched them leave until a gust of wind caused her to turn in his direction.

The cold didn't faze him as he was still running hot under the collar. He reached out to touch her shoulder. "You don't have to do this."

"I do."

"I'd rather you pack up and stay somewhere else for the night. Your safety is my priority. You said yourself there are other search-and-rescue dogs. They can find a loophole and call them in early, or you have rangers who—"

"Do you have any idea how overwhelmed search-and-rescue teams are right now? We have millions more people using public lands lately, which is great, but search and rescue is predominantly made of volunteers. They work normal jobs and have lives. They already get paged over a hundred and fifty times a year. Besides, I know the forest land around town the best. The SAR team here trains mostly around the ski areas."

"You work a full-time job, too. You never take a break, do you? It's clear the community loves you because you're serving all the time. You don't have to be a superhero, Violet. Take the rest when you need it."

"Look who's talking. You've been undercover ever since he's been gone, haven't you?" She tapped her index finger on his chest. "You and I are the only ones who understand that the world is void of all the good Rick would have done, all the lives he would have saved and—"

"Of course I understand! But just like the world, the void in your heart isn't going to be filled if you're exhausted all the time." His words rushed out, full of heat, and he instantly regretted dropping his guard when her face crumpled.

"It's all I have." She blinked rapidly. "It's me and Teddy and the only thing we know to do."

"Maybe it's time we both learn other things. Open up to other possibilities."

Her eyes shimmered in the moonlight. "I'm not sure I can."

He held his hands out. She hesitated, staring at his palms for a moment before placing her hands in his. He wrapped his fingers around hers. "I don't want to insult you by saying I know how you feel."

She glanced down at their hands. "No, but out of everyone else I know, you might come the closest."

"When I look at you, I realize I need to take my own advice. I'm weary of the undercover life."

"Does that mean you're ready to request a new partner?"

He exhaled and looked away. "I don't know. Maybe."

"I understand. Good thing we don't have to try to do it alone, right?"

She was referring to the Lord, he realized. He dropped his head, and her forehead pressed against his. He wasn't ready to pray aloud, but he knew from all the times he'd shared meals at her house that she was lifting up a silent prayer. He asked for the weariness to be left behind, for help in keeping her safe and solving the threats that seemed to surround them. He exhaled, his breath a cloud as he opened his eyes and lifted his head to find her gaze on him.

His mouth went dry. She had a small tear on the side of her cheek, frozen in place. He lifted his hand and gently wiped it away. Her lips parted, and he could only hear the pounding of his heart. She lifted her chin ever so slightly, and Alex drew her closer. He lowered his mouth and—

"Have a good night, Violet."

They pulled apart as if splashed with a giant wave of cold water. A man waved as he shuffled in the snow to a minivan.

"You, too, Darren," Violet croaked. She shoved her hands in her pockets. "I think we should go. Now."

His gut dropped as if a heavy weight

had landed in it. What had he done? Had almost kissing her ruined their friendship forever?

Teddy's snoring stirred Violet awake before her phone vibrated. The Newfoundland had located Bruce in one hour flat, so she didn't begrudge him the snores that could rival a lion's roar.

Covered in half an inch of snow, Bruce had at least been in a hefty wool coat. There'd been an empty bottle of liquor beside him and several key pieces from the gallery in his trunk. If the sheriff hadn't already seen for himself that someone had framed Eryn for the jewelry store robbery, he'd likely have hauled Bruce straight to the drunk tank. Apparently, Bruce had been trying to drum up investors, unsuccessfully, for a ski-equipment shop.

Whoever was framing her two friends had done their research. She racked her brain to think of who could want to do this, but her mind kept betraying her need to focus by replaying the moment Alex had held her in his arms. The cell buzzed again, refusing to let her ruminate. She rolled over to unplug the phone. The first text was from the sheriff:

Good news or bad news first?

She had a preference for bad news first, but the sheriff hadn't waited for her response to continue texting.

Toxicology report returned. Same as Eryn. Bruce recovering. No fingerprints on syringe from last night.

No new leads, then. The phone vibrated rapidly with a message from Eryn.

I knew it! Darren said he interrupted what would've been a five-alarm kiss. Sorry for you! Hope you still got the kiss! I'm getting discharged this morning, and

Darren is moving back in, provided our counseling appointment goes well today. Prayers, please. By the way, I heard Bruce got drugged the same as me. Is Alex any closer to finding out who's doing this?

She let the phone rest on the nightstand and fell back on her pillow, not awake enough to respond. So she hadn't imagined anything. The whole town would soon know that she'd almost kissed Rick's old partner. Thousands of tourists might be in town at any given moment, but locals still kept tabs on each other. They weren't all gossips, but if it wasn't slanderous enough to keep lips sealed, word spread. They really didn't need a newspaper, in her opinion.

Her fingers drifted to her lips. What would the kiss have been like? Her heart pounded. The thought of actually falling for Alex was terrifying for a thousand reasons she was too flustered to rattle off, but the biggest was he wasn't Rick.

Maybe she was lonelier than she'd realized. That was her own fault, confirmed by her conversation with Eryn.

Her phone buzzed yet again, and Teddy issued a warbled complaint. She rolled over to stare into Teddy's golden eyes. "Sorry, boy. No one wants to let me ruminate on my thoughts and feelings in peace this morning."

The message was from Alex.

Coffee is ready. Officially no longer undercover. Contacted campaign treasurer myself. I think you're going to want to hear what I found out.

She hustled through her routine and opened the bedroom door to smell a mixture of bacon, eggs, toast and coffee. She inhaled appreciatively. Much better than the microwave sandwich or cereal bar she usually shoved in her mouth on the way out the door. She avoided eye contact, though, when Alex turned toward her with a full mug of coffee.

"What'd you find out from Chris? That's the treasurer you meant, right?" She took a sip as Alex held up a meat stick with a question in his eyes. She nodded. Teddy deserved to have one since he'd had to give one up the night before.

Teddy gobbled up the snack greedily before moving to the food bowl that Alex had already prepped. He'd been up early.

"It's your pastor," Alex said. "He's the one that bought the tickets to the fundraiser."

"What?" Violet almost spit out the steaming liquid. She blinked rapidly. "Why would he do that? I know his salary, and it's not enough to be buying parishioners two-thousand-dollar tickets to a political event. Maybe someone else in the church wanted to gift it anonymously and went through him." Even that seemed like a stretch.

"Which is why I've set up an appointment to ask him."

"You can cross him off the list of suspects. Eryn would've recognized his voice if that's who she'd given our details to on the phone."

Alex nodded. "I did track the phone number Eryn called to RSVP to the party. Burner phone. No one answered."

"See? He's not the guy."

"But just as we learned something from talking to Eryn, we might learn something if we ask him a few questions." Alex glanced at the time on the microwave clock. "The secretary set up a meeting in twenty minutes. I thought you would appreciate getting it done before work."

"It's a good thing Teddy and I get ready fast."

"Can I ask you a personal question?"

Her heart pounded. Did he want to talk about last night?

"Why is it so cold in here all the time?"

His left eyebrow popped slightly. "Is heat really expensive?"

She snickered, surprised at the question. "Sorry. I guess I'm used to it. It's not a money-saving thing. You don't want to be around Teddy when I don't keep the house cool. Newfoundlands are kind of known for their drool."

He cringed. "Really? I haven't seen him do that."

"Because I don't let him get too hot. Embrace the cold and have more coffee." She hustled back to her room, with a smile on her face. Within fifteen minutes, she'd repacked her gear and the search-and-rescue bag and was ready to go. The moment she shut the vehicle door, though, the awkward electricity between them returned.

"About last night," Alex said. "That, uh, moment in the parking lot. I need to apologize."

Suddenly, it was hard to breathe. She really couldn't handle hearing that their almost kiss was a mistake. Of course, it was a mistake, but she didn't want to hear it from *him*. She wanted to keep her dignity in place.

"Listen. It's fine. I'm sure being undercover can get confusing. For a second, I could believe we were a couple, too." The words rushed out so fast it felt like her ribs were being compressed in a vise.

"No, that's not what I meant."

She took the corner a little faster than necessary and pulled into the church lot. "Oh look, we're here."

"Can we pick up this conversation later?"

Or never would be better. "Sure." But if Alex didn't bring it up again, she certainly wouldn't. They were just two exhausted people who probably hadn't had any real human contact in months. That was all. She exhaled, finally able to breathe freely again.

They stepped inside the church. The early morning quiet of the building enveloped her. The thick carpet and walls managed to turn down the volume even on Teddy's panting. Pastor Sean Stafford rushed toward them with his hand outstretched. "You must be Alex. Welcome!" He nodded at Teddy and Violet. "Nice to see you both again."

Alex leaned into the handshake. "I must say, I'm surprised you know who I am."

"The church secretary filled me in. She keeps her ear to the ground, as they say—"

"And she's married to Sheriff Bartlett," Violet added. She should've known.

"Let me say welcome to the community. Anyone who's a friend to Violet is a friend to us. Mindy thought you might be here to request premarital counseling?"

Her throat closed tight, and Alex had a coughing fit as he took a step back. "No. Actually I'm here on official business. I have some questions about a case."

The pastor waved toward his open office, and they took some seats. "I'd be happy to help, but I can't imagine how."

Violet pushed past her discomfort, even though her cheeks still felt on fire. "Can you tell me why you ordered tickets for Eryn and me—?"

"And Bruce," Alex interjected. He gave her a side glance. "Given the events of last night, I asked the treasurer about his ticket, as well. It will soon be public record that the pastor bought an entire table at the governor's fundraiser."

"But I didn't!" His hand rested on his heart. "There must be some mistake. I don't have that kind of money." Pastor Sean opened the front drawer of his desk, riffled through a few papers and pulled out an invitation.

"That's the same one I received." Violet fingered the paper. His didn't have a phone number or request to RSVP like Eryn's, either. "Turns out they never printed invitations, only tickets."

"I never go to anything remotely political as a rule, so I didn't attend." His forehead scrunched. "How much were the tickets?"

"Two thousand dollars a plate," Alex said. "And there were eight seats at a table."

"Sixteen thousand dollars," the pastor muttered. He waved at someone behind them, and they turned to see the sheriff through the glass wall. "Sheriff, I'm glad you came." He nodded at Alex and Violet. "I was just informed that my name was used to purchase almost twenty thousand dollars' worth of tickets, but I never—"

"And Mindy said the church is missing forty thousand dollars from the general account?"

The pastor nodded at the sheriff's question. "Very concerning."

Violet's spine straightened, and Teddy stood, no doubt picking up on her tension.

The sheriff cast her a meaningful look. "Violet, how come everyone in your circle is one of my suspects this week?"

"Su-suspect?" the pastor stammered.

The sheriff nodded. "I'm afraid so, sir. This is all causing quite the strain in my marriage, too, so we might need a marital counseling appointment after I ask you a few questions." He glanced at Violet and Alex. "Assuming you're done here?"

"I think I have a picture of what happened," Alex said.

Violet stood. "Sheriff, you know this is going to end up being like Eryn and Bruce. It has to." She stared at the pastor with new perspective. He wasn't a thief or a mastermind. Was he? No. He'd have no reason to ever hold a grudge against her or Rick. No reason to steal her husband's memorabilia.

"I'll keep that in mind. Keep me updated on what you two find, okay? I hear there's quite a ruckus brewing at the hotel."

Alex nodded as if he knew what the sheriff was talking about, but she walked in a sort of fog back to the vehicle.

"What's the motivation? Why would someone want all of us at that fundraiser dinner?"

"The simplest reason would be to make sure you were all out of the house."

"That only makes sense if they already intended to also frame every one of us from the beginning." They both settled back into their seats, and she started the engine.

"Perhaps we should rethink this from the beginning."

"It all started with Rick's stuff being stolen. His college stuff..." Her mind was trying to make a connection. It felt like she was reaching out and trying to grab a memory, and she'd almost found it...

The radio in her SUV burst her concentration. "Ranger Sharp?" One of her law enforcement officers rattled off his handle. "You've been requested out at the hotel immediately by Tom Curtis. He says it's an emergency."

She shifted into gear before he signed

off. "Buckle up." She flipped on the sirens before speeding out of the church parking lot. Her gut was tied up in knots. There was only one reason Tom Curtis would call her in an emergency. The one person she cared the most about in the entire valley was also the closest she'd ever come to having a daughter. "I think Daniella is in danger."

NINE

Alex stiffened. Violet's adoration for Daniella had been written all over her face every time she'd spoken of her. Whoever was tormenting her had to know that.

"I hate to sound like a broken record," he said. "Whoever is doing this knows way too much about you. Are we sure that your ranger recognized the voice on the phone as Tom's?"

Her gaze darted his way before returning to the road. "He's local. Of course he would. Why would you suggest that?"

"This morning—"

"The 'ruckus' the sheriff mentioned." She took a sharp inhalation. "What do I not know, Alex?"

"I was going to tell you, but I figured

we'd discuss it after I had more information. My supervisor dispatched more FBI agents here after our conversation about explosives last night."

"But I told you the snow ranger hasn't confirmed any theft, and the troopers already know—"

"That's not all. This morning, the security cameras picked up a man running through the halls with a black bag over his shoulder. It had an orange emblem that read Danger. Explosives. They're evacuating the lodge as we speak."

Her foot slipped off the gas pedal, and the SUV slowed drastically as they ascended a hill. Her entire face scrunched. "Even if we do discover the explosives were stolen, we don't carry them in bags like that."

Exactly. And Alex also didn't need to explain that the Firecracker would never be spotted so easily. "Given that the security cameras were compromised last night—"

"Whoever is trying to get my attention is better at sneaking around than the Firecracker or..."

"Or someone wanted to make sure the footage was seen to lure everyone out. They wanted the hotel to be evacuated, which is why I'm concerned you're being called there." His heart beat faster. Rick should've never died rounding the corner of that building. The FBI had ruled Rick as a casualty of an assassination attempt gone wrong, but Alex had never understood why there were bombs at that location in the first place.

His mouth went dry. What if the Firecracker and Violet's tormentor were one and the same after all?

"Violet, I know you didn't want to cause Teddy any undue anxiety after the vet last night, but what about now? I think it will be best if we get you relocated. Someone's already been in your house once."

She refocused on the road and took the final turn he knew would lead them to the hotel. "Someone came into the house while Teddy and I weren't there. If they really know that much about me, they'd know I'd have the advantage in my own home."

"They tried to get you outside a hospital, Violet. And going to the hotel now might be walking straight into a trap."

"If someone wants to talk to me that bad, maybe I should just get it over with so all of this will stop."

He held his tongue. She couldn't really mean she'd *let* them kidnap her. Worry led people to make impulsive statements. After they found Daniella, he'd try again. Maybe even get the sheriff and friends to help convince her to move to a safe place before this escalated even more.

She took another corner without slowing down. The sudden motion didn't faze Teddy. The special seating behind them had been made with high-speed pursuit in mind, or maybe he was so heavy that nothing moved him when he didn't want to be moved. As they approached the hotel, the traffic turned into gridlock.

"Like I said. They've started to evacuate already."

"The entire hotel?"

"They're checking every single room with the K-9 bomb dogs. Once they're sure there are absolutely no devices, they'll allow guests back in. I'm sure there will be some who won't want to return."

She flashed the siren and was able to get around the bottleneck and into the parking lot, though it was pure chaos with lines of cars waiting to leave. Violet swung up onto the curbside. It would be the best spot out of the way.

As they ran toward the entrance of the resort, Alex kept his FBI badge out in hopes they'd be able to get closer. Violet pointed out Tom. His tie was loosened and dress shirt untucked. He was directing employees and pointing at groups of wide-eyed guests with their luggage. He stiffened at the sight of Teddy, held up a hand at the people waiting to speak to him and ran forward. "Violet, I'm so glad you're here. With all these strange things going on, I knew you'd understand the urgency. It's not like Daniella to disappear. She's not like that anymore."

"And security footage?" Alex asked.

"They said it's missing."

Alex exchanged a dark look with Violet. He would need a word with the FBI immediately. They were trusting security footage as reason to evacuate the hotel, and yet it didn't work whenever they actually needed it. He leaned over to speak with only Violet. "Someone wants everyone out of the hotel. We need to consider why, and we need to assume it's the Firecracker running the show."

Her eyes flashed. "Right now, the only thing I'm considering is Daniella's safety. Tom, I need something personal of hers. Can you get something out of her employee locker?"

"They won't let us back in."

"I'll see what I can do." Alex flashed his badge and pointed to the lobby.

The other agent shook his head. "You need to take that up with the special agent in charge."

He was ready to argue there was no time, when Violet interjected, "Tom has run to see if there's something of hers in their car. They carpooled together to work." Her attention shifted to his jacket. "Do you still have that photo? The one that someone stuck in Teddy's vest?"

He pulled it out of his pocket, struggling to focus while radioed messages were exchanged between officers from multiple agencies. "I don't see how this can help right now."

Violet took the photo, flipped it over and held it out to Teddy. "Ready to work?" The dog sniffed the photo wildly. "He knows my scent, so he'll ignore that." Teddy lifted his head upright and swiveled toward Alex, pressing his nose into his pant leg. "Right, he's got you now. Which leaves…" Teddy sniffed the back of the photo again, and this time, his back went rigid.

"Go to work," Violet said gently.

Teddy dropped his nose to the ground and spun in a circle.

"You don't think Daniella's scent is on the photo, do you? She can't be the one behind all this."

The dog's fluffy tail turned rigid, the tension coming off him almost electric. "No, of course not," Violet said, her eyes riveted on Teddy. "But I think he might've caught the scent of whoever has been toying with us, and I assume that person is the same one who took Daniella."

Teddy vaulted forward.

"He has something!" Alex said.

"Yes." Violet jogged beside Teddy, her attention on protecting the dog in the busy parking lot.

Alex rushed forward. "You focus on the dog. I'll keep you two safe." He held out his badge and waved the other hand to block the line of cars trying to get down the lane and out of the lot. The dog darted right, and Alex sprinted ahead to block a second row of cars.

The dog stopped, turned around in three circles, then slowed his pace. In Alex's peripheral vision, as he was holding traffic back, he could see the slump of Violet's shoulders. Maybe Teddy wasn't so hot on the trail anymore. Or perhaps the person had driven off somewhere.

Teddy stopped abruptly, touched his nose to the back of a black SUV and sat down.

"She might be in here." Violet rushed forward, her hands cupped around her eyes to peer into the darkened windows.

"Stop. Step away." Alex ran over for a closer look. A federal license plate. This was the vehicle that the future nominee for the Federal Reserve chair would be traveling in. "Get Teddy and go back to the resort. Now."

"What? No. Daniella could be in there."

A blinking light caught his eye. Alex took a knee and peered under the SUV. His heart stopped beating for half a second. He had to get Violet away from here, or they'd all be dead.

Violet let loose a shout as Alex lifted her up into the air. She fought against the instinct to take him down. Her head bobbed violently as Alex ran. "Let me—"

He dropped her to her feet. "Only if you keep running. I saw a bomb, Violet. Bomb."

"Daniella..." Her name caught in her throat. "Why didn't you let me look inside first?" She pressed forward, but Alex blocked her. Teddy shoved his head in between them, as if trying to act as a referee. "Just let me check for her." Horns from a few of the cars blared as they were still blocking the lane.

Alex held up his badge at the closest window and placed his other hand on her shoulder. "We need a SWAT team. Even if she's in there, you don't know if the doors are rigged or if someone—"

The black SUV transformed into a ball of fire before her eyes. The shock wave shoved her backward to the ground. Her head stung, but she flipped over instinctively, hands over her ears, mouth open. A second later, a cacophony of car alarms started, and the earth stopped shaking. Teddy licked her hand. She rose to her hands and knees and gazed into his eyes. "Are you okay, boy?"

Her own voice sounded like it was coming through a sock. Alex's blood-tinged hand dipped in front of her face, offering help. She pushed herself upright, not wanting to cause him pain. She wasn't sure which one of them moved first, but they were wrapped in each other's arms. A pop sounded in her eardrums and the car alarms and sirens tripled in volume. Painfully loud.

"I'm so sorry," Alex whispered into her hair. "I've done it again."

She had no idea what he was talking about. One name ran through her head over and over. Daniella. Daniella was likely dead because of her, and she didn't even understand why.

"Medic! Doc! Somebody!" A man's shouts pulled her attention. Tom jumped up and down, waving toward the front of the hotel, desperate for assistance.

"Why is he calling for help?" She straightened. "Why is he calling, Alex?" Hope reverberated through her entire being. If he wanted a doctor there, at his car, then maybe... She began running with Teddy by her side through the parking lot, ignoring the acrid smell of smoke stinging the back of her throat and eyes.

Tom caught sight of her. "It's Daniella. She's unconscious. I need help!"

A shuddering breath overtook her, and her steps faltered. Alex grabbed her arm, keeping her from a fall. "She's alive, Violet."

Tom likely thought she looked like a lunatic, because she couldn't stop smiling even as her vision blurred. Unconscious meant alive. Daniella was alive!

Violet darted through the spaces between the cars and reached the blue Subaru Forester, with Teddy right on her heels. She yanked the passenger side door open to see Daniella sprawled across the back seat. Tom was on the other side of the car, his door open, as well.

She reached for Daniella's wrist, and a strong pulse hit her fingers. She lifted her face to the sky and mouthed her silent prayer of thanks.

"What is it?" Tom pressed. "What's wrong with her?"

"She's likely been drugged with a sedative," Alex answered. "She'll need to be taken to the hospital, but if she's like the other cases, she'll recover fully. I'll make sure the EMTs head this way!"

"Other cases?"

Violet wasn't sure where to begin. Her throat burned with tension as she took another look at Daniella. The floorboard was filled with trinkets from the gift shop. Tom stooped down to look inside, his eyes full of torment. "She wouldn't have started shoplifting again. That's ridiculous. Why would she jeopardize her future once more?"

"She didn't, Tom. Someone set her up. I don't know why it's happening, but I think someone wants to get to me by hurting those I care the most about." Teddy stuck his head in and nudged Daniella's hand. There was no movement except for the steady rise and fall of her chest to convince them she was still alive.

Violet's stomach vibrated with the tension. Daniella had been so close to the bombing. Too close. What if Tom's car had been next to the one with the bomb? "I'm so sorry. This is because of me, but

I won't rest until I stop whoever is doing these things."

Tom's forehead creased in confusion, but he didn't reply. Alex returned and touched her arm. "The paramedics are heading over now. I know you want to see if she's okay, but you have to let others take care of her."

She stood so Tom wouldn't have to witness what was sure to be an argument. "I can stay out of the way of EMTs, but I want be here for her when she—"

"No." Alex's face had a white pallor, and it appeared as if he was going to be sick. "Don't you see? Teddy found the scent of the person who slipped the photograph under his vest. The same person who is so determined to torment you. The one who bombed that SUV. Do you understand what I'm saying?"

She shook her head. The pieces that snapped together in her mind had to be wrong. They had to be. The bombs had been placed in that SUV by an assassin.

The Firecracker. "But why?" She hated the way her voice sounded small and afraid.

The paramedics jogged past the car in front of them, headed their way. Violet, Teddy and Alex stepped out of their way. The movement helped her see clearly. People who were still on the premises had gotten out of their cars, some crying, some hugging. Was it out of fear or relief that Alex had kept them from driving any closer before the bomb ignited?

"I don't know why," Alex said. "We're going to figure it out, but right now, I need to get you somewhere safe. He's targeting you, and you can't be out in the open like this, Violet." He glanced over his shoulder where Daniella was being lifted out of the vehicle and placed on a stretcher. "She's going to be okay. The sheriff will ask her if she saw anything. Let's go."

She was a target. His words bounced around in her mind. If she was a target, then anyone close to her might get hurt. Alex was in that photo. He'd be next.

"Violet? Can we go now?"

She nodded and let him lead her and Teddy away from the scene. She barely registered when he asked for her keys, got her and Teddy in the car, and weaved them through traffic, taking alleyways and side streets before parking in front of her place. Once inside, she made sure Teddy drank extra water before she sank onto the couch. Teddy leaned against her shins and placed his enormous head on her lap, staring into her eyes. He thought she needed comfort, but for once, he was wrong. She felt numb.

A plate full of salad appeared in front of her. The last thing she wanted to do was to eat.

Alex sat beside her and offered a smile at Teddy. "Sorry, buddy, but I didn't think you'd be too jealous of our salad."

"I have responsibilities, people to help. I can't let the Firecracker—"

He rested a hand on top of hers. "Take five minutes to eat and try not to think. We have a long day ahead of both of us. Let's refuel before we argue about next steps."

Her lips twitched. There was something comforting about being with someone who knew her well enough to know they were about to disagree. She jabbed the fork into a heap of chopped spinach and romaine. The food tasted like dirt, though. Whether it was due to her emotions or the choice of rabbit food as a meal, she couldn't tell for sure. "I appreciate it. Though I'm eating this under protest."

"You and Rick had the most prepackaged diet I've ever seen. I used to worry you'd both end up with scurvy."

"We weren't *that* bad." She stopped to think about her normal diet. "Okay, maybe we were, but after a long day of work, neither of us wanted to do the cooking."

"Understandable, but I'll feel better if I leave here knowing you have had some real food. You'd probably grow to like it, you know."

"I knew you were an optimist."

His smile disappeared. "Listen, before we move on, I really need to get this off my chest. I should never have even wanted to kiss you—"

His words were like an electric jolt. Instead of being numb, she wanted to run. "Alex. Please. We don't need to discuss it." She couldn't help that her heart skipped a beat at the news he'd wanted to kiss her.

"We do. I've been trying to work up the nerve to tell you this for over two years." His voice caught, sending apprehension down her spine. "It's about the night Rick died. An informant told us the Firecracker was scoping out a building. When we arrived, Rick was supposed to take the west side." He hesitated and dropped his head. "But I knew he had better aim with more sunlight, so I told him to switch places with me."

She struggled to follow what he was saying. "Better aim?"

"We were clearing the perimeter before backup arrived. When Rick rounded the corner on the east side..." Alex closed his eyes and took a deep breath. "There shouldn't have been explosives there. The target would've never gone that way, but—"

"There was a bomb," she finished for him.

"It should've been me. I told him to switch places with me. It was my fault."

She stared at the broken man in front of her, but his declaration was too overwhelming for her to offer him comfort. "Why?" Her question came out in a whisper. "Why are you telling me this?"

He shook his head but avoided eye contact. "Because I could never kiss you without you knowing it was my fault he's gone instead of me. And today you were almost killed, and I can't help but think it was my bad judgment call that…" He inhaled sharply and shook his head. "I just needed you to know."

But she didn't want to know! She stood up rapidly. The right thing to do was to tell him that it wasn't his fault, that she didn't blame him. The only reason he'd told her was because he wanted to feel better. Now, every time she looked at Alex, she'd think *if only…*

"I'm sorry. If I could go back in time, I would change places with him." The regret on his face was real.

"What's done is done." She strained past the throbbing in her throat. "You were right. It's not safe here. I'm going to pack." She needed to be alone, or she'd never be able to think straight.

Teddy lifted his head and looked between the two of them. The most expressive dog she'd ever known, his eyes were wide as if to say, "What should I do? Who needs comforting most?" She held her palm out flat, a sign he could stay. She walked down the hall and closed the bedroom door behind her. She didn't want either of them to see what was sure to be an ugly crying session.

Lord, why? She dropped to her knees by the side of her bed and dropped her forehead on the cool sheets. *Chaos.*

That word yet again. She wiped the escaping hot tears from the corners of her eyes but kept them closed. Her memory heightened. Sitting in the common room on orange bucket chairs, the criminal justice study group staring at Bridget after her declaration. "Chaos is the answer," Bridget had said. "Stretch limited resources thin and—"

"So now we all know who to come looking for if you decide to go to the other side and show criminals the *right* way to go about things," Rick had responded with a smug grin on his face. That had been mere days after he'd broken things off with Bridget, and weeks before he and

Violet would have their first date. The group had laughed at his comment, and Bridget had narrowed her eyes.

Violet opened her eyes and stared at the light blue walls and the metallic print of the mountains hanging on her wall. Bridget was the type to hang on to perceived wrongs for a lifetime, the type to want to torment Violet. But she was dead. She was dead, wasn't she?

A shadow crossed the metallic print. She moved too late, just as one man clicked the lock on her bedroom door while another came at her with a syringe.

TEN

Alex hadn't meant to cause her more pain. He was sure she was missing Rick with renewed intensity, and she wasn't the only one. He used to sort through his problems with Rick. Not that Rick was one to beat around the bush. If Alex stuck his foot in his mouth, Rick had always been quick to say, "Fix it."

He smiled at the memory. Ironic since this mistake had to do with Rick, and there was no easy fix. His go bag was almost ready, he just needed to repack a few things so that he'd be ready to leave soon. Thumping above, followed by grunts resounded through the floorboards.

Alex glanced at the ceiling, but he wasn't going to fall for that again. She was working off some frustration and anger with her martial arts. Not a bad idea. He felt like punching a few boards himself. Maybe he should've never told her. He certainly didn't feel any relief or newfound peace after having done so, but he'd felt the need to let her know for two years.

She wouldn't want to see him again for quite some time, maybe ever. His fingers shook as he tried to fold his last shirt. Once he got her to a secure location, he was going to hand her security off to another FBI agent. He just needed to convince his boss that she needed protection. The harder job would be persuading Violet that she and Teddy couldn't respond to any search-and-rescue calls for a while. A tall order.

No casualties from the bombing at the lodge were reported, but it had been a close enough call to send the Federal Reserve chair nominee out of town. The welfare of the nominee was out of his hands now, but the FBI would be searching the records of all the Federal Reserve Police to see if they could track the mole there. Given the Firecracker's old-school method of handing over flash drives, Alex doubted they'd find anything.

Teddy barked incessantly, followed by more thumping. Maybe the dog was taking it personally that Violet had closed her door for some privacy. Alex came back to Rick's words before his death. *Something about this is starting to seem familiar.* If it was familiar to Rick, maybe it was something personal. Alex stared through the window at the thick blanket of fresh snow covering the mountains.

Bridget Preston had died, but what if she had made it abundantly clear what the Firecracker should do to never get caught? What if one of the students in the criminal justice study group had taken up the cause? But it couldn't be a copycat case because of the DNA they'd found.

Teddy burst through the door at the top

of the stairs, his weight flinging it open. It hadn't been locked, but the movement stunned Alex. The unusual behavior combined with the sound of breaking glass shot adrenaline straight to Alex's heart. He bolted up the steps. Teddy turned and ran ahead of him, jumping and launching his front paws at the bedroom door. "Violet?"

More breaking glass could be heard. "Help!" Her call was hoarse and followed by a grunt.

"Teddy!" Alex swung his arm behind him. The dog understood and shuffled backward. Alex kicked his foot directly below the knob, and the door splintered, swinging open.

Violet face was bright red. An arm wrapped around her neck. She elbowed the man behind her and tucked her chin underneath his hold, slipping out of his grasp. A gun lay on the ground behind the man she'd just struck, but another gun was on the floor in front of the second man, who was currently doubled over in pain. Despite the man's groans he bent over farther, and his fingers were mere inches from the gun.

Alex rushed forward to stop him, but Violet slammed a sidekick into the bending man's back. She spun and issued another kick into the stomach of the man she'd just managed to free herself from. Teddy's deep growl set Alex's teeth on edge as he managed to grab the gun on the floor. He heard rapid footsteps and another bark.

He looked up just as Teddy launched himself at the other man who had just drawn his weapon. The dog grabbed the collar of the man's jacket in his jaws and brought the man down with him as he landed back on his paws. The gun hit the ground and slid underneath the bed.

Alex raised the weapon he'd retrieved and aimed it in the direction of both men. "Enough!"

Movement out the window in his peripheral vision briefly distracted him. A woman in the trees, pointing a—

The window exploded.

"Violet!" Teddy let go of the man's jacket and moved in front of Violet. She crouched to the ground, and Teddy flopped down, his paws sliding underneath the bed, but his head was clearly too big to fit underneath the frame. Bullets pinged the wall as Alex ran over to cover Violet. He only half registered that he didn't see where either of the men had gone before he crouched over her. The moment the shooting stopped, he prepared to return fire. He lifted his head to find the men were no longer in the room, and there was no one visible outside the window.

"I think they ran out the same way they got in," Violet said, breathless. "Through my bathroom, past the walk-in closet."

"Stay down until we're sure the shooter outside is gone." Alex still had one of the men's guns in his hand and his own Bureau-issued one at the back of his waist. He peeked over the edge of the mattress. The woman in the tree was no longer there, but she could be waiting at another location. He ran through the closet, checking to be sure they weren't hiding behind the clothing, and into the bathroom. The window above the tub was wide open. He raced to it, gun raised. There were two hooks over the windowsill, attached to ropes dangling all the way down to the ground. They swayed in the breeze.

A house situated next to the woods provided privacy, but the downside was neighbors couldn't see anyone approaching, even in the light of day. The rev of engines sounded, and from behind a grouping of trees, three snowmobiles took off. Two men and one woman, all with helmets on, darted through the trees and headed toward the foothills of the mountains behind the house.

"Whoever shot up the bedroom is gone."

Violet stood in the closet, a gun in her hand and Teddy at her side.

"They took off on snowmobiles." He took note of the scratch on the side of her face, the hair that had escaped her ponytail and the sweat gathered on her neck. "Are you okay?"

She leaned over, her hands on her knees, still catching her breath. "What took you so long?"

"Let's just say 'message finally received.' You can take care of yourself."

She coughed a laugh, and her eyes grew misty as she straightened.

"I actually thought you were practicing martial arts before Teddy came and got me."

"You came just in time. I practice for a group attack, but I was starting to make mistakes. My gun was in my nightstand, but they caught me off guard." She patted Teddy's head. "Thanks for the assist."

She lifted a piece of fabric from the dog's mouth and waved it in Alex's direction. "Teddy made sure they won't be getting away this time. Let's go."

Violet led him to the snowmobiles she had parked in the side garage. They were both outfitted especially for Teddy. Usually, she kept one at work and one at home, but on the last late-night mountain mission, she'd snowmobiled straight home for a good night's sleep. She threw a set of keys at Alex and pointed at the helmet. "You've ridden before?"

"Yes, but I think we need backup."

She flipped on the communication in his headset and set it to her shared signal. "Agreed."

Violet picked up her radio and requested backup from dispatch. They'd send one of her law enforcement rangers first, as the forest was on federal land. The snowmobiles were equipped with GPS tracking. "Have him follow my location." She signed off, checked Teddy's harness, and slipped on her own helmet. "At this rate, it'll be hard to catch them. Every second matters. Let's go."

She cranked the ignition and started following the path through the trees. This part wouldn't require Teddy, but if they lost the trail or came to a highly trafficked path, that's where Teddy would take over. The clouds were gathering in the sky and casting a gray pallor over the valley that made it harder to see.

"Can you hear me on this thing?" Alex's voice came through the speaker in her helmet.

She focused on steering around a snow pile that could be covering a small tree. "Yes."

"Now might be the time to let you know I've only ever ridden on marked trails."

"You need to stop telling me things when it's too late to do anything about it." The tension in her shoulders continued to build.

He exhaled through the speakers, and

it sounded like he was blowing air into her ears.

"Sorry," she added, knowing he was thinking about Rick's death again, as was she. "This just seems like our best chance to catch whoever is doing this. I'm tired of people I care about becoming targets."

"Noted," he said. "Any snowmobiling tips I should know about?"

She stood up on the running boards as she took a sharp right. "If we're cutting across hills, use the throttle control and your body position to keep the tracks pointed where you want to go. Never ever stop halfway when you're going up a hill." She hesitated. "Unless it's on a sharp cliff where there could be a snow bridge ready to tumble."

"Should I stand up?"

"Only if you feel it helps. I have to do it to compensate for Teddy's weight." She leaned her entire body to the right while keeping her left foot on the running board to make another sharp turn and then settled back on the seat. Her little side mirror revealed the dog happily in his harness.

She had to focus now on the tracks in front of her. So far, the three sets from the other snowmobiles were easy to follow. They were nearing the crest of a hill she knew would be safe, but the snowpack was deeper now, making it more dangerous. "Too much throttle, and you'll drive too deep into the snow, Alex. Too little makes it harder to balance."

"So, no pressure is what you're saying?"

She rounded the top and slid slightly to the left. "Pop the throttle and countersteer."

Alex huffed in her helmet. "At some point, no amount of maneuvering is going to win over a five-hundred-pound heap of metal and the forces of gravity, but I'll do my best."

Fair enough, but she had to think positive while driving with Teddy behind her. The trees cleared out on the next stretch they ascended. A gust of wind blew a light dusting of snow over the tracks. The lines were still visible, but if there was any more snow, she'd need to stop and ask Teddy for help. On a clear day, the expanse of white, much like an empty canvas, would've taken her breath away. Racing across the snow was the closest she'd get to flying, with the occasional bouncing on clouds.

The trees disappeared, and in the distance, boulders and spires poked out from underneath the thick snow like icebergs. If they made a wrong move through the snow here, it could be fatal.

Only one track remained in front of her. Odd. Either the three people had merged and followed the exact same grooves—unlikely—or a pair of them had peeled off. A gust of wind indicated that snow had covered up the trail of the other two.

"Is it just me, or has it gone eerily quiet?"

The engines of the snowmobiles were

anything but quiet, but she knew what Alex meant. The sky held no birds, and without trees or other signs of life, she and Alex were exposed. She pressed forward, and boulders rose up on either side of them, offering protection. It felt like being in an alley, except with rocks instead of buildings. The air grew still, no longer blowing gusts of wind.

Was this what being hunted felt like? As if someone was holding their breath, waiting for her to enter into their shot. The space between the rocks narrowed. The carpet of snow resembled a runway leading straight up to the top of the hill.

"Something doesn't feel right," Alex said softly.

She agreed. Even if she was wrong, she didn't want them to crest that hill and find themselves on a sharp decline without protection. "There are some spaces between the boulders up ahead. Let's split up. You go right. I'll go left. Keep heading due north without topping the hill. I'll find a way to round it at an angle from the other side. Maybe we'll cut them off."

"Affirmative."

She stood and placed all her weight on one of the running boards. The sweat from the afternoon's events dripped down her back. Even if she hadn't spent ten minutes fighting off two men with weapons, this type of snowmobiling tested her abilities. Thankfully, they'd practiced it enough. Teddy had learned how to counterbalance with his head, as well.

They made the turn smoothly. She could see the crest of the hill now. With precise movements, she maneuvered to take it at a diagonal. As they reached the top, she saw someone wearing a white snowsuit standing on one of the spire tops, red hair spilling out the back of her helmet. The woman lifted a rifle, pointed at them and pulled the trigger.

Violet swung the handles, making a hard left to avoid getting shot. The snow gave way several inches, and the snowmobile choked, throwing her off. She flipped head over heels and landed on her back. Snow kicked up from every side. She flung her arms and legs out to slow down, but hitting a mound of hard snow took her breath away.

She was sliding down the hillside head-first at high speed with nothing to stop her but boulders that could take her life. Teddy was skidding mere feet from her, on his back. She fought to spin around so she could see what dangers lay below them, but before she could, something far worse entered her vision. The snowmobile was rolling, bouncing, and heading straight for them.

"I've spotted the men. I'm going after them! Violet?" She heard Alex calling her name through the helmet, but she couldn't answer. She twisted, straining her neck and every muscle in her back until she caught her gloved fingers on Teddy's harness. She kicked a foot out and yanked him toward her, narrowly avoiding the tip of a rock jutting out. Each bump they hit slammed the breath out of her lungs. The snowmobile caught air, lifting up and over them. If it fell on them—game over.

The ground disappeared from her back, and they dropped into thin air. She lost her grip on Teddy's harness, and her hands and legs flailed until she slammed into what felt like a cement slab. Her feet started to sink, and an icy, wet abyss rose up around her. Water poured into her helmet. She felt Teddy's paws against her chest. She blinked rapidly, and the bubbles in the helmet moved enough to see his eyes staring into hers.

A current forcefully thrust them to the side and abruptly changed direction. She was being dragged under by her foot. The snowmobile had dropped in the lake with them, and her foot was caught on the machine.

The frigid waters numbed her body. Teddy was free and floating to the surface. She closed her eyes, and the moment hit her with clarity. If she had told Alex to go left instead of right when they split up, he'd be the one at the bottom of the lake. She understood now the burden he carried. Too bad she'd never have a chance to tell him.

Sleep offered relief to her burning lungs. If only something would stop pulling so hard on her arm.

ELEVEN

Alex swerved, narrowly avoiding plowing the snowmobile directly into a boulder that came out of nowhere. The two men on snowmobiles were getting away, darting through another bunch of trees on the far side of the hill. His snowmobile stalled from the sudden decrease in speed. He slammed his hand on the front of the seat. He'd lost all contact with Violet. They never should've split up. He tried again to reach her. "Violet?"

He stepped off the snowmobile, and his leg sank a foot into the snow. He turned, searching for Violet. Over his shoulder, to the west, a woman with red hair flying out from the back of her helmet and a rifle strapped to her back stood on top of a spire. She paid no attention to Alex or the men on snowmobiles. She was staring at the lake down below.

Below her were two tracks that... Alex's stomach lurched. The tracks disappeared into a wide berth of disturbed snow that led directly to the lake. The lake... Teddy's head broke the surface and then disappeared back under.

"No!" He grabbed his weapon and spun back to the woman, but she was gone.

He shoved the snowmobile with all his strength. *Lord, if ever I needed help, it's now!* He pushed again, and the snowmobile mercifully slid two feet. Alex hopped back on and cranked the motor. Seconds. He only had seconds to get all the way down the hill to the lake and find her. His entire body trembled as he fought to make smart decisions, weaving his way toward the water. He'd be no help to Violet if he crashed. He hit the radio and called for dispatch. "Where is our backup?" His voice croaked. "District Ranger Sharp is down. Medic, we need a medic. Shooters in the vicinity."

He hit a snow divot and momentarily lost control, sliding sideways down the steep run. Remembering Violet's words, he popped the throttle and steered against gravity, standing and leaning in the opposite direction. Mercifully, he came around and straightened. Only a hundred feet to the alpine lake now. The first ten or twenty feet of it had to be solid ice, but the interior section of the blue waters was still visible.

As he reached the ice, he flung himself off the snowmobile and rushed forward. His shoes had little grip as he skated his way to the water. The helmet cast aside, he fumbled for the zipper of his jacket, removing the layers as fast as he could to prepare to dive. The dog's head crested the water as he reached the edge of the ice.

"Teddy!" A hand. The dog held Violet's hand in his mouth. Her helmet bobbed on the water as the dog's powerful strokes headed his way. Never before had he seen a dog's paws work the way Teddy's did. The webbed paws created a current of water rushing behind him. Violet's helmet may have broken the surface, but he didn't know if her nose and mouth were out far enough to breathe. Her body was still immersed in the water.

Within seconds, the dog made it to the edge of the ice. Alex slipped his hands underneath her arms. "I've got her, Teddy." He straightened and fought against the slippery surface to pull her up and onto the ice. The last thing they needed was to both go under. The frozen surface held, and he gingerly laid her down. His fingers shook as he fought to unbuckle the helmet first. The water had already drained from the inside, but as he pulled the gear fully off her head, his ribs tightened at the sight of her blue face. He fought against nausea as his stomach lurched.

Teddy entered his peripheral view, shaking water off his fur. The dog rushed toward Violet, and those golden eyes held the same question that was on Alex's mind. Was she alive?

Alex dragged her by the heels until they reached the solid snow. Rivulets of water ran from her hair and hands. Opening her mouth, he forced all emotion to the back of his mind. He moved her head back and tilted her chin to start resuscitation. She gasped. Her eyes flew open. She twisted to the side, coughing as her entire body began to shake violently.

He knew too much about drowning. No water had been expelled from her mouth. So either her body had fought against the water by forcefully closing her airways, or her lungs had absorbed the water. There was a serious risk anytime the brain was deprived of oxygen, but there was also the danger of the lung tissue swelling and filling with fluid. Alex had no idea how long she'd been under before Teddy pulled her to safety.

They hadn't prepared the snowmobiles with any emergency first aid gear before they left, at least not the one Alex had been driving. He grabbed his coat and wrapped it around her. The woman exuded strength when conscious, but at this moment, she seemed frail and delicate.

She was still wet, but layers had to help. She didn't fight him as he lifted her into his arms, confirming she needed a hospital right away. Even though she was out of the water and breathing, she was nowhere near being out of the woods, both literally and figuratively. Teddy ran alongside him to the snowmobile. The sleigh designed for Teddy was big enough for the Newfoundland and Violet. "I'm counting on you to keep her warm, boy."

The dog rushed forward and slid down next to her without prompting. Alex pushed his hands into his fur to confirm the dog was bone dry underneath his top coat. Amazing. Her eyes flickered open and she groaned.

"Hug him, Violet. Hug him tight. I'm going to get us out of here."

She wrapped her arms around Teddy and buried her face into his fur. How long she'd have strength to do so, he didn't know. And would he even be able to find his way back to town without Violet leading the way? He had to at least try.

A snowmobile crested the mountain top to the east. Alex froze. One lone man sped directly toward him, gliding over the snow. Teddy jumped up to all fours and barked in that direction, but it seemed without animosity. Alex kept his hand on his gun until he realized the man wore a green jacket. A USFS jacket.

The man flipped the front of the helmet upward as he got closer. "I'm Ranger Alatorres. Are you injured?"

"No. I think they shot at Violet, and she ended up in the lake. Teddy pulled her out."

He nodded at the dog. "Where are the shooters now?"

"Two headed west. The other one, I have no idea." Alex pointed at the spire behind him. "She was stationed there with a rifle." He glanced down and realized Violet was unconscious again. Her bluish skin hadn't improved.

The ranger jumped off his snowmobile and ripped open a white packet. He shook an orange square of folded plastic rapidly, and it puffed up. "It's a heated emergency blanket." He unwrapped it and tucked it around Violet. "Better than nothing. We're working on getting more backup here. I need you to head due east. Air ambulance will be landing there any minute. Avalanche risk is too high for them to get any closer to the mountains behind me. Follow me."

Alex didn't hesitate. He'd lost his helmet somewhere near the icy water, so the wind stung his face as he pressed into the breeze and bounded after the ranger. Helicopter blades in the distance confirmed the ranger's words, but Alex feared they might be too late.

Violet's feet and hands had never felt so warm, which didn't make any sense. Her lungs weren't burning anymore, either. Wasn't she in a lake?

"I really don't think the nurse is going to approve." Alex's voice came through her mental fog like a bright light.

She blinked to find Teddy resting on her feet. Alex was leaning over her bed, holding both of her hands between his own warm palms. His attention was focused on her dog, though. "I'm serious, Teddy. If they want to kick you out, that means I'd have to take you, and I'm not leaving."

"Teddy, off," she croaked. Oh, maybe that was a mistake. Her throat didn't enjoy speaking.

Alex flinched and straightened. "You're awake!"

Teddy got off her feet, but the dog attempted to squirm into the small space between her body and the bed rails. He didn't fit. His head reached past her hip, though, and the way his golden eyes widened made him appear so concerned. "I think I'm fine, boy. Can I get some water, though?"

Alex lunged for a nearby stand and brought her a cup of water with a straw. She eagerly drank, and Teddy, seemingly satisfied she was okay, finally hopped off the bed as a nurse entered the room.

The woman raised an eyebrow and huffed. "If you hadn't saved her life, you'd be out on your ear, K-9 hero status or not."

The water took away almost all the pain in her throat. "He saved my life?"

"Along with a few other people," the nurse said, nodding at Alex. "Glad to see you awake." She reached for Violet's hand and placed a device on her finger. The screen illuminated, and the woman smiled. "The doctor will be checking on you shortly, but your oxygen levels are back to normal. We'll need to watch you a bit to make sure you don't have any complications, and then you'll be free to go."

Her memory was slightly fuzzy, but Violet remembered the woman with the gun and the snowmobile barreling after her and...

"Whoa!" The nurse shook her head and tapped a monitor next to an IV bag. "Let's think calm thoughts to keep that heart rate down. In fact, let's check that blood pressure." As the nurse grabbed a cuff and slipped it on the arm without tubes attached, Alex approached the bed.

"That's a tall order," he said.

"Borderline high." The nurse hooked the cuff back to the wall. "Keep the conversation light." She leveled a serious glare at Alex and Teddy before smiling at Violet and leaving the room.

The memory of the water filling her helmet, and her foot being caught, surfaced. "How did Teddy get me unstuck from the snowmobile?"

"You were stuck?" His jaw clenched, and his skin paled.

"A spring had me caught."

"You were missing a boot when I pulled you out." He leaned over and rubbed behind Teddy's ears, and the dog's back right paw went wild, gently shaking her bed. "I guess your inspiration wall really influenced him."

"I told you he has those instincts. And we train in water rescue weekly. It's a little humbling that he doesn't need me to get it done."

The dog made a harrumph noise before he flopped over to the side. He was likely more annoyed that Alex had stopped scratching behind his ear, but the timing made her wonder.

"I think we both need you." Alex's face flamed. "I mean, we need you to be okay." He cleared his throat. "I know you're probably pretty upset with me still."

Her heart rate monitor was bound to bring a nurse back in soon. He was referring to their conversation before those men had attacked her. That moment at the bottom of the lake wasn't one she wanted to relive, but she understood why Alex had needed to tell her. He moved to stand, his shoulders hunched as if carrying a physical burden of shame, and she reached for his hand. He stiffened, but his eyes softened, searching her face.

"It was my call, my decision to go left through those boulders. I told you to go right. Imagine if I'd told you to go left. You don't have as much experience on the snowmobile, especially a large one equipped like that. And you wouldn't have had Teddy to rescue—"

"Violet, you can't—" He froze in the middle of shaking his head. His forehead creased, and he seemed to be fighting off waves of emotion.

She held his hand tighter, desperate to make sure there was no misunderstanding each other. "You were going to tell me that in law enforcement, you can't second-guess every decision, weren't you?" She pressed forward before he could answer. "I saw the information in front of me, everything in front of me, and I had seconds to react. By God's grace and the training I had to rely on, I made the best decision I could."

Alex turned his face toward the door and started to pull away. She placed her other hand underneath his. "Please, Alex. Hear me on this. I don't need your forgiveness. For all we know, if you had switched places with Rick, both of you could've died that day." Her voice broke. She had to accept the unknown to find peace again. Otherwise, the what-ifs would destroy them both.

His chest rose and fell, and she felt his shuddered sighs as if they were her own. Teddy rested his head on Alex's foot. Alex lifted his chin, looked at the ceiling and blew out a long breath. "Thank you, Violet."

"Thank *you* for saving my life."

He turned toward her.

She blinked rapidly, willing the blurriness away, and an awkward laugh escaped.

His face morphed into a giant grin. "I'm always surprised when you laugh and cry at the same time."

That made her laugh again. She wiped away the tears at the corners of her eyes. "I think I work so hard to hold back my emotions that when one breaks out, they all come out at once."

"All of them?" His hand brushed away hair from her face.

Their eyes locked. "Yes," she whispered. The noises of the hospital faded away as Alex bent over so their faces were mere inches apart. He hesitated before his lips brushed against her cheek.

A knock at the door pulled him upright. Focusing on the doctor at the threshold instead of the keen disappointment weighing on her chest proved a challenge. She barely heard the doctor's questions or registered as he listened to her lungs and told her she could leave after a few more hours of observation. The side of her face still felt warm from where Alex had kissed her. Why did it feel like he was trying to say goodbye?

The chaos of the week began to flood her mind. The moment the doctor left the room, she turned to Alex. "Before the men broke into the house, I'd started to wonder if Rick's death was intentional, personal. Bridget was obsessed with the profile of a perfect criminal. Chaos was her solution. If a criminal used minor crimes to thin out law enforcement resources, the bigger crime would go off without a hitch."

"She thought the Firecracker was the perfect criminal?"

"No, she thought he could be. She thought the Firecracker's work was the cleanest, the most sophisticated. She admired him. Whenever she got like that, Rick would break the tension by joking that if a criminal started doing what she'd suggested, we'd know to come look for her."

Alex sat down in the nearest chair, his mouth agape. *"Something about this is starting to seem familiar..."*

"That's almost exactly what Rick said to me."

"And me," Alex said in hushed tones.

"Was their chaos like that when Rick was...?" She hated to ask questions about his death, and yet it was a relief to ask someone who might actually know the answers.

Alex's eyebrows jumped. "Yes. Police were overwhelmed that week with a string of robberies." He shook his head. "But how likely is it that someone would remember college—?"

"You didn't know Bridget. She was always suspicious, downright paranoid sometimes. She insisted those qualities would make her an excellent detective."

"She was right, to a point. I've already asked the FBI to reevaluate the copycat angle. We should look at the professor who gave your group the case files to study and any other member of your study group."

"I know it's a long shot, but it might be worth a check."

He hunched over, staring at the floor. "Arrangements have been made, Violet. I'm being called back in."

She stiffened and averted her attention to the ceiling. "Back to the Salt Lake office?"

"Yes. I put in a request before you woke up. I thought you wouldn't want to see me again."

"Obviously, that's not true." Her words came out in a whisper, straining against her tightening throat. She reached for her water and drank, hoping it would relieve the tense emotions, as well.

"I'm doing my best to convince my boss that what's happening with you this week is connected to the Firecracker, but I don't have enough evidence." He gripped the arms of the chair and squeezed, his knuckles turning white. "Since the future Federal Reserve nominee has left, they figure the danger to you has left, as well."

"No evidence? You must be joking. The bombing at the parking lot—"

"The explosives were stolen from the ranger shed. Your snow ranger confirmed that. But I'm trying to tell you that we have no proof of any connection to the druggings and the—"

"What about the laser scope I saw?"

"That's not the Firecracker MO." He exhaled. "We both know someone has it in for you and everyone around you, but we don't have proof it's related to the assassination attempt. It's just conjecture." He splayed his fingers wide, set them on top of his knees and leaned forward, finally looking at her. "Would you consider moving to Boise?"

The question jolted her. She set down the water. "What?"

"It's only a couple of hours away. You'd be close to the Boise National Forest, so you should be able to transfer, under the circumstances. It has a big enough population and plenty of small towns nearby to start your search-and-rescue school."

She studied his pleading expression. Was he trying to tell her he was going to move to Boise, too? She knew the FBI had an office there.

"Your family is there," he added. "Your mom and sister, right? And there's more law enforcement. A city would be safer."

The taste in her mouth turned sour. He just wanted to get her safety off his conscience. He was leaving, and whatever brief wonderings she'd had about a future together vanished before her eyes. "Will you go back to undercover work?"

He twisted his lips to the side. "Trying to change the subject?"

She shrugged.

"No," he answered.

"I thought you still have a couple undercover cases you're working."

"I was taken off those so I could follow the Firecracker lead my informant gave me. They'll turn my absence into rumors of my demise."

"Is it that easy to fake a death?"

His eyes darkened, and he shifted in his chair. "People see what they want to see, hear what they want to hear," he said softly. "I've been wanting to check with the officers who responded to Bridget's car crash and find out more about her death, as well."

The change in subject was a welcome one. She wasn't ready to discuss leaving Sunshine Valley. "I think that's a good idea." The thought that Bridget could've gotten away with faking her own death horrified her. Bridget on the loose without accountability... She'd either be a vigilante or worse, much worse.

If Violet agreed to move to Boise, the people she left behind might be safer, but what if she brought the danger to her mom and sister? The thought of her family brought her mind back to Daniella. Last thing Violet had heard, the girl was still unconscious. "Is Daniella in the hospital? I'd like to see her."

He nodded slowly. "She woke up a few hours ago. I actually need to ask her a few questions."

Daniella had been drugged and helpless in her dad's car, so close to that bombing. And all because of Violet. She dropped her head into her hands. The past couple of years, she had worked so hard at being okay, at staying busy, at living life without needing others. Now she saw that existence as the lie it was. The people in this town were near and dear to her heart, and she'd been fooling herself to believe that she could live without love again. But it was clearly too late.

"I'd like to get dressed and go with you," she said. "Go ahead and make those calls. The faster you do, the faster you can pack up and leave, right?"

He pulled his chin back, then slowly nodded before leaving the room. She hadn't forgotten that Alex's image had also been circled in the photograph. He'd be the next target, she was certain. If they couldn't find the person doing this, she'd never be safe again and neither would anyone she cared about. The faster Alex left, the better, for the sake of his safety and her heart. But if he left, would they lose the only chance that remained to finally capture Rick's killer?

TWELVE

Alex left a message with the Jerome County sheriff's office. The deputy who'd first reported to the scene of Bridget Preston's crash into Snake River Canyon would call him when he reported to his next shift. Patience wasn't Alex's strong suit. He wanted there to be easy answers, but then there was a matter of the DNA left at previous assassinations. They'd even found the Firecracker's DNA at the scene of Rick's death. Could Bridget be working with the Firecracker? The thought that the mysterious assassin could be training others to follow in his footsteps would keep Alex up at night.

Violet stepped out of the hospital room dressed in the extra USFS uniform from her go bag that the rangers had dropped by the hospital when they delivered her vehicle. The level of respect the team had for Violet was obvious in the few minutes he'd spent answering their questions on her condition.

He'd known she was an amazing woman for years, but after holding her in his arms, he couldn't stop thinking of what it would be like to be more than friends. That dangerous and uncomfortable mind-set meant he needed to leave town as soon as possible.

Violet tilted her head, studying him. "Everything okay?"

"Yes. No news to report. Waiting on a call back." He gestured with his phone to the end of the hall. "Daniella's room is at the end on the left."

She worried her lip before turning in that direction. The small gesture drove him to distraction. She bit her lip when she was trying not to say something, he felt certain. She never used to do that, at least not that he'd noticed. He made her uncomfortable, and yet he had gone ahead and kissed her on the cheek. He blew out a breath, mentally kicking himself.

Tom sat in a chair by the door, as if serving as a guard. He glanced up, a scowl on his face at the sight of them. Violet winced.

"Tom, I'm so sorry for what happened."

"You didn't do it," Daniella spoke from her hospital bed. "They didn't, Dad."

Tom grunted but remained silent and returned to his book.

"You're awake." Violet beamed at Daniella. "I was so worried about you."

"It was super weird, but I'm totally fine. I'm mostly mad I didn't get to see the SUV blow up for myself. Everyone knows I was there, and yet I can't tell them what it was like because I slept through it."

"Someone drugged you."

She rolled her eyes. "I'd rather not

tell people I was drugged, thanks. They might get the wrong idea."

Alex took out his badge and held it out to Tom.

"State troopers have already asked her questions," Tom said. "She didn't see anything. Is this really necessary?"

Alex nodded before moving to Daniella. "I'm afraid I need to ask you some more anyway. I'll be looking at it from a different angle than the troopers. Walk me through the minutes you remember right before things went dark."

"Did you see who drugged you?" Violet rested her hand on top of Daniella's shoulder.

Daniella nodded. "No. I mean, I didn't see who did it to me. I was in the parking lot. It was early and still dark, because winter is the worst." She spread out her fingers. "I was about to start my shift but had forgotten my gloves, so I headed back to the car. I saw the reporter, but I don't think she saw me. Then everything went dark."

"What reporter?"

"Um, I forget her name. A woman who writes for *Sunshine Valley Weekly* or something."

"The troopers weren't interested in the reporter," Tom added.

Alex tried his best to smile and nod at Tom, who was clearly agitated. "Could you humor us, Daniella, and tell us more? Do you remember her name?"

"No, but I met her a month ago, so I think she's legit. She was waiting outside the forest service office when I locked up one afternoon." She hesitated and gave Violet a side-eye.

"Why was she there?" Violet pressed. "The smallest details might actually be important."

Daniella blew out a long breath. "Well, it's going to ruin the surprise, but fine. She said you were going to be named Sunshine Valley's person of the year. She just needed to ask a few questions to fill out the piece she's working on."

Alex pursed his lips, pretty sure there'd be no such honor given by the *Sunshine Valley Weekly*. He rapidly typed a set of searches in his phone's browser. Nothing.

Daniella huffed. "Look, she wasn't a scam artist or anything. She already knew all about Rick, and she wasn't creepy. She wanted to know what I liked about working with you—"

Violet offered her a warm smile. "You told her I was your mentor?"

"Yeah. I told her you were somewhere between a big sister and a second mother. Maybe more like a cool aunt."

Alex put away his phone. "Do you remember what she looked like?"

"Long hair. Some shade of brown, but it was totally a wig. I didn't ask her about it or anything. Didn't want to be disrespectful, in case she had gone through cancer or something, but it wasn't the shade for her."

"How'd you know it was a wig?" The courier at the party had black hair, the woman at the restaurant had blond hair and the reporter had brown hair, but maybe they were all the red-haired shooter. He couldn't allow himself to start making assumptions at this stage yet.

Daniella eyed Violet. "Do you want to tell him, or shall I?" But Daniella didn't give Violet a chance to answer. "I style hair for free for my friends. Have my own video channel. Might own a salon someday, but I'm exploring my options. Want to be wise about my skill set and all that."

Violet beamed, and Alex once again felt like his heart was about to explode. He loved seeing the way these two interacted, and he couldn't help but imagine how Violet would be as a mom. Or a cool aunt.

"Was that it, Daniella? Did the reporter ask you anything else?"

"No. I think that was it."

Alex turned to leave.

"I mean, other than asking who else she should interview about Violet."

He spun around. "She asked for more names?"

Violet's eyes were wide. "Did you give her any?"

"I gave her Eryn's name and Pastor Stafford's. I thought they could give better lines than I could. I mean, the best story I could tell about you was how you won the church's hot-dog-eating contest, and then you wanted a bag of chips and soda to finish the meal off." Daniella used air quotes for the last four words. "But I didn't tell that story."

Violet's face turned as red as he'd ever seen it. "I don't normally eat like that."

Daniella smirked and turned to him. "You really need to help her start eating like a human. I worry about her health."

"Working on it," he said with a nod. "I took her to your dad's restaurant for starters."

Tom grunted in response but made no

comment. Tom would likely need to be out of the hospital and days from the bombing before he'd be able to smile again.

"Hey! I'll have you know, I ate a salad today." Violet scowled. "Feels like that was a week ago. It's been a long day."

"To be fair, after living a day in her shoes, I can see how she's been able to eat like that and get away with it." Alex wasn't ready to admit how sore his core was after maneuvering the snowmobile in rough terrain. If Violet wasn't complaining, he certainly wouldn't. He tapped his phone where he was making notes. "You gave this reporter Eryn and Pastor Stafford's names. Anyone else?"

"No. She asked me about Bruce, out of the blue, which I thought was weird since that was so high school, but she wanted his last name."

Violet turned to Alex. "That'd be all she needed."

His mind raced. This woman had been

in the area for a month, asking questions. Was it possible the events at the political dinner had nothing to do with the Firecracker? Impossible. His phone began vibrating. He looked to Violet, who nodded. He trusted she knew what questions to ask as he stepped out to take the call.

"This is Deputy Griffon. I heard you want to know about Bridget Preston's crash?"

"Yes. You're the one who found the body?"

"No. The body was never found. It was high-water days in Snake River Canyon, but trust me, after falling from the cliff into the river, and judging by the state of her vehicle, no one could've survived that."

Alex felt like punching a wall. "Unless she wasn't in the car at the time." His voice was strained from the tension.

"We did our due diligence, sir." The deputy addressed him with a patronizing tone. "There were witnesses from the crash. Two men, I believe. And part of the flannel she was seen wearing that day was left behind, snagged by a broken window."

"Windows don't break easily."

"They do if remnants of a tree go right through them."

"Thank you for your time," Alex said softly, though his mind was churning over possibilities. "One more quick question. Do you have the names of the two men who witnessed the crash?"

"Uh, yeah, but they were tourists driving through." The deputy went silent for a couple minutes and then rattled off two names, one that ended in Smith, and the other that ended in Johnson. Most likely fake, but Alex jotted them down to have the Bureau trace them.

"Can you remember what they looked like? Specifically, how they carried themselves?" Alex was careful not to lead the deputy, but if he described the men as being two broad-shouldered, wrestler types, they were on the right track.

"It was winter. They had coats on. I really don't remember much."

Alex signed off but jotted more questions on his phone's notepad. Based on his conversation with Violet, combined with Rick's last words, Alex needed to re-evaluate the Firecracker's work since he'd reappeared back on the scene. They had DNA from recent cases that was a partial match to the assassinations from twenty years ago, and that had been enough evidence to rule out a copycat. The Bureau had stopped looking for any other differences. Did the hits in the past ten years that they'd credited as the work of the Firecracker also have strings of unusual crime surrounding the timeline?

Violet joined him in the hallway, her eyes wide. "Teddy is the evidence."

"What are you talking about?"

"You said you needed concrete proof to convince your boss that everything happening in town is connected to the assassination attempt. Teddy found the scent on the photograph and led us straight to the SUV. You said it yourself after the bombing."

"Well, yes, but…" Was she right? Was the dog enough?

"Teddy is the evidence," she repeated. "He's a K-9 trained in water rescues, avalanche rescues, and certified in search and rescue." Teddy panted with his tongue hanging out, as if he knew he was being praised. "While we don't work criminal cases, his nose will hold up in a court of law, so it should be good enough for your boss." She eyed him. "Is it enough for you to stay and bring down Rick's killer?"

His heart pounded in his throat. An hour ago, she'd acted like she couldn't wait for him to pack up and leave. She'd seemed to have forgiven him for his part in Rick's death, but then mere moments after that, her eyes had grown distant and cold. Like hanging on to a roller coaster by his pinkie, he couldn't keep up. If Rick were here, he would've told Alex that was because Violet's emotions were impossible to read. How many times had Rick complained about that very thing? Alex had to be certain. "Are you sure you're okay if I stay?"

"After hearing Daniella talk about the reporter, I know we've got to be close to ending this. We might finally have some answers."

"No, that's not what I mean." It was now or never. He had to lay his fears on the line. "Do I bring you pain, Violet?"

Her hand flew to her stomach as if he'd thrown a surprise punch. The pupils in her eyes grew wide. "Why? Why would you ask that?"

"Because I remind you of Rick. And I know you said I have nothing to apologize for, but that doesn't mean that it doesn't hurt when I'm around."

"No. I mean, at first maybe, but now..." Her eyes had a sudden sheen to them.

Was this one of those times where all the emotions were trying to escape, or was she trying not to hurt his feelings? He'd imagined she'd see it as a betrayal to Rick to send him away.

The compulsion to press wouldn't be ignored. "I guess I'm wondering if we can ever be friends, just you and I, without Rick." He cringed, unsure it was fair to have voiced his thoughts aloud.

Her mouth dropped, but a second later, she straightened, appearing ready to answer until her gaze flickered above his shoulder and darkened. The sheriff strode down the long hospital hallway.

"You here to ask Daniella questions, too?" Alex shook his head ruefully. "We should've scheduled appointments. We were round two of questions for her."

"That's not why I'm here." The sheriff pressed his lips together in a firm line and stared down at Violet.

She tilted her head back and groaned.

"Please don't tell me another person is missing."

"Also not why I'm here. Though maybe I should be asking you if there will be any more missing persons."

"What?" Alex placed his hands on his hips. What was the sheriff implying?

The sheriff sidestepped Alex until he was right in front of Violet. "Given the circumstances, I'd say it's past time for me to ask you some questions."

Violet offered a half-hearted laugh, but she looked over her shoulder into Daniella's room before addressing him. "Ask away, Sheriff, but maybe tone it down before you make me sound like a suspect."

The sheriff slid his hand an inch toward his holster. "I'm afraid I can't do that."

Violet paced in her own hospital room. At least the sheriff had been willing to move their conversation here. Teddy paced alongside her, despite her assurances that he could sit down. He was keyed up in a way she'd rarely seen, especially when he should be exhausted after rescuing her from the icy lake. He kept his gaze on her face and was clearly worried about her, then. She stopped and patted his head so he would relax.

"Maybe this should wait until Violet has a lawyer present." Alex stood in front of his chair with his arms crossed.

"I'm not taking her in or accusing her of anything. Not yet."

This would be a lot more comfortable if the doctor would discharge her. She was fine. News of the sheriff coming to the hospital to interview her like a suspect would go through town like wildfire. "I have nothing to hide, so let's get it over with. What are your questions?"

"What do Eryn Lane, Bruce Wilkinson, Pastor Stafford and Daniella Curtis all have in common?"

She sank into the edge of the hospital bed. "I think you already know the answer to that. They all know me, but they all know other people in this town."

"It's a known fact that house values have been skyrocketing in this area. Word is your mama is gonna kick you out."

Violet barked a laugh. "Sheriff, do you need my mom's phone number?"

"Where did you get your information?" Alex asked.

"The rental never has guests because that's the way you like it. That's also common knowledge. Maybe you're desperate for funds to buy the house."

"I'm a paying guest," Alex said. "And what happened to no accusations? She committed the robberies and framed all of her favorite people while she was at it?"

The sheriff shifted uncomfortably.

"Where are you getting your information?" Violet asked. "The same place you heard stories about Eryn and Bruce and—"

"Like I said, I'm not accusing you of anything yet."

"No offense, Sheriff, but I think we have different definitions of what *accusing* means." She was sure of one thing, though. If the sheriff was spouting this as common knowledge, then that meant this theory had become town gossip. They needed to locate the person who had fanned the flames of the rumors.

"Violet, you're the only one who's connected to everything happening in this town." The sheriff took a step closer to her. "It's my job to get to the bottom of why. If you're holding anything back, now is the time to let me have all the facts."

"You could start with Daniella," Alex said. "She will confirm that a so-called reporter showed up at Violet's place of work, claiming the *Sunshine Valley Weekly* was planning a story on Violet. The reporter needed the names of those closest to Violet. That's your missing link. We find the fake reporter, we find the person behind this. Eryn Lane also had to respond to a sham RSVP for the political fundraiser. When I tracked the number, I found it was a burner phone."

The sheriff turned to Alex and narrowed his eyes. "Is the FBI working on these drugging and robbery cases, as well?"

"Not officially, but I have reason to believe that the same person responsible for all of those things set the bomb today and the bomb that killed my partner."

"Rick?" The sheriff took a step back. "Does the FBI have evidence to back that up?"

"Teddy," Violet said.

The sheriff cringed. "As much as we love Teddy, I was hoping you'd have a little more than that."

Before Violet could educate the official on the validity of her argument, a cheery nurse entered, staring at her clipboard. "Good news!" She lifted her head, read the room and her demeanor shifted into seriousness. "Your final test came back normal. The doctor gave me the go-ahead to start discharge papers. Sign these, and you're free to go."

The sheriff moved to the hallway. "I'll check into this reporter. Stay in town, Violet. You'll be going back to the house or work?"

"She'll be staying at the hotel," Alex answered.

"The hotel?" While she'd resigned herself to not sleeping in her own bed until they'd captured the gunmen, she found the choice surprising.

He turned to her. "After the bombing, they have quite a few openings. I got us adjoining rooms. There are enough troopers still working the scene that I feel it's our safest option in town." Alex gestured at the sheriff. "You must know someone is trying to target Violet, as well. I saw the gunmen myself in her house. A third person shot out her window."

"At your house?" He swiveled to Violet. "Why didn't you file a police report?"

"I called dispatch to send my rangers in pursuit of the men. Maybe I wasn't as clear about why I was pursuing them." She gestured at her arm and the bright pink bandage covering up the puncture from the IV. "I've been a little busy. I'll file a proper report with my rangers as soon as I leave, as the incident happened on forest service land."

"I gave Ranger Alatorres the gun one of the men left behind at the house," Alex said. "He was going to run prints, which I assume happens in collaboration with your office."

The sheriff nodded and crossed his arms over his chest. "I heard about what happened at the lake. My understanding is no one has been found."

His tone set her teeth on edge. Was he insinuating that he didn't believe her? "Alex can corroborate my story. I didn't crash the snowmobile into the lake for fun."

"I'm glad you're okay." The sheriff shuffled toward the hallway but stopped at the door. "I didn't know about a shooting at your house. Resources are stretched pretty thin right now, as you know, so I'll go there and gather the evidence myself."

"I appreciate that."

He nodded before turning away. "I'll be in touch."

Alex stared after him. "Do you trust him?"

"Should I trust anyone right now?"

He looked wounded. "Fair point. Shall we go?"

"Gladly." She reached for her go bag, but Alex picked it up first.

He held up one hand. "I get just how capable you are, but I'd like to help."

"Thanks. After today, I'm not turning down any rescuing." Her cheeks heated, and part of her regretted that she'd been unconscious when Alex had helped her to safety. He must have carried her in his arms.

Alex exhaled a shaky breath. "You'd think in my job I'd enjoy rescuing, but I hope I never have to do it again."

She walked down the hallway with Teddy at her side, mulling over his words. What did he mean by that? If Rick had said something similar, she would've taken it to mean he hoped he'd never see her in danger again. But with Alex, she was unsure. One moment, she thought there was a spark. The next moment, she thought he was kissing her cheek goodbye for good. And then what was all that about being friends? The question still hung in the air since the sheriff had interrupted them. Maybe it was a small mercy, because she had no idea what to say to him yet.

She pulled her shoulders back. How could she think straight about him when he was right next to her? Alex only wanted to be friends and was worried about bringing her pain. Busy and fulfilling work had been enough in her life until he'd walked in and showed her that she wanted more. More than friendship.

She inhaled sharply and put a hand to her chest. The truth was, being *only friends* with him would be painful. Would Alex ever be able to understand that, or would he think she was betraying Rick's memory?

"Violet, are you okay?" Alex reached for her shoulder, his own steps slowing to stay at the same pace. "You're flushed. Should I get a nurse?"

She blinked rapidly. "No. If someone is still out there, I'll never be free to have friends or anything else," she added quickly while her courage ran hot. "They said someone wants to talk to me. If this is personal, my mind keeps coming back to Bridget time and time again."

Alex hesitated. "There's a possibility she's still alive."

"I knew it."

"I don't want to give you false hope, though." He raised both his hands, as if trying to slow her growing optimism. "It's best we revisit all the facts to figure out other possible suspects."

"Is there something you aren't telling me?"

"They never found her body. The officers think she was swept down Snake River."

"What if she was never in the car in the first place?"

"They had two male witnesses."

Violet couldn't help but laugh. "Two guesses who they might be. The woman on the spire… If she's also the reporter, Daniella would be able to identify her. I think I have a photograph of Bridget." If they could put a face to Violet's tormentor, this could all end. Every law enforcement officer in the area would be keeping an eye out for her within minutes.

Alex raised an eyebrow. "A photo? I thought all your photos were stolen?"

"Just the ones I kept at the house. I have a bin of other photographs in the storage unit. It's a long shot, but I think I still have some from those early college days there, a time before Rick. I know my mom took a photo when I first met my roommate at move-in day. If we have a photograph of her, we might have a photograph of the current Firecracker."

Alex's face lit up. "Lead the way, partner." The air grew heavy with his words. "I... I was being flippant. I'm sorry, Violet. I've stuck my foot in my mouth so many times. I'm so sorry."

She forced a smile. His words confirmed he would never see her as anything but his partner's widow. "It's okay. I know you must miss having a partner." She patted the side of her leg as she started down the hall, and Teddy matched her pace. "I know I rely on mine."

THIRTEEN

Alex's cup of coffee had gone cold. After a mostly sleepless night, he now sat on the floor, his back to the threshold of their adjoining hotel rooms. The trip to the storage shed had yielded two plastic bins full of Violet's college memories. They'd spent hours sorting photographs into piles last night, but they still had no leads this morning. Teddy snored from on top of the closest double bed.

Violet worked on the other side of the room with her bin. They'd agreed to sort photographs into two piles. The photographs with Violet alone or with only males were placed to the side. Photographs with females were in another pile. Alex was to keep his eye out for anyone that looked familiar. So far, nothing had registered.

Flipping through favorite moments in Violet's life amused him, though. Here in all these photographs was the woman Rick had fallen in love with. His gaze paused on her beaming smile, her bright eyes. He looked up to see her stretch across the room and grab another piece of pizza.

"What?" she teased. "I ate those carrot sticks first, like you asked."

"No judgment here," he said.

She rolled her eyes in dramatic fashion before taking another bite. He laughed but couldn't take his eyes off her as she moved back to sorting photographs. This wasn't the same Violet that Rick had married. Sure, there was a lot there that was still the same, her kindness and compassion and brilliance, but grief had changed her. Grief had changed him, as well.

That difference alleviated the guilt he was fighting for being so drawn to her.

They could have never been a couple until they'd become these different people. What was he thinking? She wouldn't even agree to be his friend. He had no right to think of her that way.

"Alex!" She kept her head down, focused on a photo, shaking her hand his way. "Come here. I think I've found something."

He jumped up as she stood and shoved a photograph his way. "Recognize anyone here?"

Violet and another young woman with a curly mass of brown hair stood side by side in front of a room with twin beds.

"Is this Bridget?"

She nodded. "Ages ago. On the first day we met. Does she look familiar?"

He studied the photograph. She could be the woman he'd seen, but he wasn't sure. "I would recognize her profile, I think, but I can't really tell from this..." He squinted at the photograph. Was it her?

Violet dropped into a chair, dejected.

"That might be the only good picture I have of her. Probably the only one that was ever printed. I think I got rid of the rest. I wasn't too fond of my memories of her by the time I graduated."

"Understandable. What about yearbooks?"

She shook her head. "No, Rick was the only one who got college yearbooks. I was too cheap for that, and I thought candid photographs were the way to go. Rick wasn't much for using his camera."

Alex laughed, but it sounded as hollow as he felt. He could probably count on one hand the number of photographs he'd taken in college, but he was pretty sure he was in several group pictures, mostly taken by his female classmates. The tension wasn't going to go away until they had a conversation. "Violet, about yesterday..."

She stilled. "I'm not ready to talk about anything personal until I'm sure you're safe."

He pulled back. "Until *I'm* safe?"

"Yes."

"Violet, the last person I'm worried about me."

"Maybe that's the problem! Have you forgotten you were drugged once and almost drugged a second time? I'll never forget hearing that gunshot..." She shook her head. "I don't need another man I—I..." She stood and walked away to the other side of the room, staring at the floor. "I don't need another man I care about getting killed."

She cared. He hadn't realized he was holding his breath. He took a step closer to her. "Do you feel responsible for me just because I was Rick's partner?"

"That's like asking if you've been watching out for me just because I was Rick's wife." Her fists flew to her hips, and she faced him, uncertainty flashing in her eyes. She seemed to deflate. "I mean, that would be a good enough reason."

"You think I'm here simply out of duty? Maybe it started that way, but Violet—" The hotel phone rang, and the shrill noise broke their connection and his courage.

She bit her lip and walked across the room. "Hello?" Her spine straightened as stiffly as Teddy's when he found a scent. Alex covered the space in three steps and leaned close to overhear what was being said.

"It's been a very busy week for you, hasn't it?" the voice asked.

Violet's knuckles tightened around the receiver. "Oh, probably not as eventful for you, Bridget."

A laugh rang crystal clear. "And there it is. What I've been waiting for."

"You wanted me to know it was you," Violet said. The phone was shaking in her hands. Alex reached up and placed his hand over hers. She turned and faced him. He held up his own phone with his free hand and texted the state trooper stationed at the security desk of the hotel.

Violet followed his thumb's movements.

Trace the call currently happening in room 303.

"This makes it so much more fun for the both of us. You may not have Rick's mind, but I figured by now, even *you* would piece it together. With the help of your fake boyfriend, of course. Is he there right now?"

Violet's face transformed from angry to panicked. "Let's keep this reunion about you and me, shall we?"

"Now, that's a good idea. Especially since you're fully recovered from your polar bear swim. Let's get together and reminisce," Bridget said.

"There's a police station I would be happy to show you. We could catch up on old times there. I'll meet you in five minutes."

Bridget laughed. "I had something else in mind, but maybe we'll try your way.

Looks like I better get going. See you soon."

The dial tone grated on his nerves. He let go of Violet's hand as she replaced the receiver. "What do you think she meant? There's no way she's turning herself in."

A knock at the door made them both flinch. Teddy barked, which was unusual for him but likely a reaction to their agitation. Alex beat Violet to the door, his hand on his weapon as he looked through the little glass window. "It's the sheriff. Do I have to open the door?"

She sighed. "Afraid so."

The moment Alex opened it, the sheriff looked over his shoulder at Violet. "I need to take a look in your storage shed. Either you voluntarily show me or I get a warrant."

"Bridget." Violet exhaled. She closed her eyes for a second. "I have a feeling I've been framed for something. I just don't know what."

Alex wanted to slam the door on the

sheriff, but that would only make the situation worse. "Wait for the warrant, then."

She shook her head. "Whatever is there now will still be there later. Time is not on our side, so let's just get this over with." She turned to grab her coat and slipped her feet into her boots. "Bridget got off easy the first time she tried to destroy me. I never thought she would go this far, but she won't win." She stared into his eyes, and he fought against the impulse to pull her into his arms. "We can't let her win."

"Don't get me wrong, I'm glad you're not putting up a fight, but I am surprised you don't want to know my reasons," the sheriff said.

"Oh, believe me, I do," Violet answered. "I just know I'm going to prove they're all wrong."

"I'll be glad if you can." He harrumphed. "I had a tip called in that you've been seen on security cameras making numerous deliveries to your storage unit this week."

"Is that so? I was there last night with Alex, and there was nothing out of the ordinary."

"Video footage looks pretty convincing."

Alex laughed. "The same type of video footage that convinced law enforcement to evacuate this hotel, which only brought people closer to danger?"

The sheriff's face reddened but he ignored Alex. "I'm here as a professional courtesy, Violet, to make sure this is done right. I could've sent one of my deputies to bring you in for questioning first."

"Understood. Let's get this over with so I can clear my name." She picked up the photograph of Bridget and handed it to Alex. "Take this to Daniella, and see if she can make an identification."

"Teddy and I are coming with you to the storage unit first. Then you can ask Daniella yourself." The forced optimism in his voice confirmed her worst fears. Bridget was a puppet master. How could the woman hate her this much from their time in college? Was it really all about Rick? Until this moment, she'd only half believed the possibility that Bridget could really have set the bomb to hurt Rick. Even now, she wasn't sure she could admit to herself that someone they'd known could've murdered him.

The drive to the storage shed took only a couple of minutes. Alex got a text and grumbled as he read it. "They were able to trace the call in the hotel room."

"Burner phone?"

"That's the theory. But I've also got good news." He smiled. "Teddy's nose won my boss over. They're sending more agents here tonight to go over everything that's happened this week, from a new perspective. We're going to get her this time. As soon as I've got a team here, we will cover every inch of the national forest with the help of your rangers, and we're going to end this. If Daniella can identify her as the reporter, Bridget Preston will be considered the suspect in an assassination attempt. She won't be able to run."

Her heart lifted, but she was so overcome, she wasn't able to speak. Bridget had been one step ahead of them for too long.

"Help is coming," Alex said, as if understanding her need for encouragement. "This time is different."

She pulled into a parking space. "You won't mind if you're not the one to personally get her?"

His smile was unwavering as he opened the car door and stepped out. He looked over his shoulder. "As long as Rick's killer is brought to justice and you're safe, I'll be happy."

Would he go back to Utah afterward? Her mouth refused to ask the question, though.

"I expect gloves to be used," Alex told the sheriff, who was waiting by the unit. The sentiment was smart, but Violet knew

Bridget would never be dumb enough to leave fingerprints. After all, only the Firecracker's DNA had been discovered at Rick's death. If this was all connected, how had Bridget pulled that off?

The sheriff entered the PIN code that Violet rattled off, and the door opened. Diamonds glittered in the morning sunlight. Artistic renderings of the valley along with abstract and impressionist paintings were displayed on top of her covered furniture. A cash box sat ajar with dollar bills sticking out.

"A little overdone," Violet muttered. Despite expecting this was what she was going to face, she still felt her cheeks heat. "Sheriff, you know this isn't me. Do you really think I would use the people I know and care about like this?"

Voicing the question aloud brought her a new sense of horror. That was what Bridget wanted—she wanted all the people Violet knew and cared about to suspect she'd used them.

"It's a little obvious, but I still need to do my job. Surely, you can understand." He nodded as he clicked his radio and asked for backup. "We're going to need to catalog all of this for evidence. Looks like roughly half of everything that's been stolen."

Her mind was still going a million miles a minute, and she barely registered the sheriff's words. Bridget would find vindictive glee in the obviousness of the frame, yet she would want to make sure the charges stuck. How would she be able to do that, though? Even Bridget had to know that Violet wouldn't stop until her innocence was proven. If the woman was the assassin, though, and had been able to plant the original Firecracker's DNA at other assassinations, maybe Violet wasn't giving her enough credit. If she could only figure out what Bridget had planned next.

"Now can I call a lawyer for you?" Alex held up his phone.

She nodded weakly. "Joanne Piper. Though she's not a criminal lawyer, she can probably get me one." A deputy pulled up behind them. The sheriff shifted his hand to his holster where his gun and handcuffs were stored.

Her stomach flipped at the gesture. "That isn't necessary."

"I'm going to have to take you in, Violet. I know this looks rotten, but the more you cooperate with me, the easier this will be."

The last words she exchanged with Bridget replayed in her mind. She turned her attention to Alex. "I told her to meet me at the police station."

"And she said she'd try it your way and would see you soon." His look darkened. "Sheriff, be on guard. I know it's an election year, but even you have to see this doesn't add up."

The officer's nostrils flared, but he refused to acknowledge Alex. "The station is the safest place in town. If you're innocent and we do this right, we can find the real culprit faster. Do I need to use the handcuffs?"

She'd never been so glad her mother and sister no longer lived in the same town. They would've surely been targets, as well. She held up her hands. "I'll go peacefully." How long would it take to ever live down such mortification? She had a feeling Bridget's plans were far worse than simple embarrassment.

Her K-9 stepped in front of her shins with a grunt, effectively blocking the sheriff from approaching. "He's only doing his job, Teddy." She reached for her keys and handed them to Alex. "Take care of him, please. You should probably hold on to his leash. If you have to go back to Utah before I'm released, get Ranger Alatorres to take over his care and training." Her eyes grew blurry. Why did she feel like this was the last time she would ever see Alex and Teddy?

"Of course, but I'm not—" His eyes

widened. "Your phone, Violet. Unlock it and let me text Daniella the photo. It'll be faster."

"Enough talk. Let's go," the sheriff said.

Violet shoved her phone into Alex's hands before the sheriff began reciting her rights and the charges. He opened the back door of his SUV and placed his hand on the back of her head to keep it from hitting the roof as she climbed into the hard plastic back seat. Teddy barked, growled and released the most sorrowful wail of a howl she'd ever heard before. How did he know she was going away?

The door closed with a slam, and she saw them through the small squares of wire in the windows. The sheriff slipped into the front seat and started the vehicle. "I really am sorry. I have a feeling my wife won't talk to me for a week after this."

She didn't feel like alleviating his guilt, even though she knew he was doing his job. When she'd picked criminal justice as a major, she'd never once imagined herself being hauled off. Her vision blurred as they drove away from Alex and Teddy. She kept her gaze on them as her ribs constricted so tightly she thought she couldn't breathe. Her heart had just come alive again, only to be ripped out and left behind.

"Please have someone check for bombs at the station before you bring me in." Her voice croaked through the tension. She was ready to face the same death as Rick. She'd imagined what it must have been like for him more times than she cared to admit. *Please don't let me leave this world without stopping her first.* The simple prayer was all her mind could handle as they drove through the forest-lined streets out of town toward the county station.

"You really think this fake reporter is the same person who killed Rick?"

The sheriff's radio burst alive before she could answer. Message after urgent message fired one after another without a pause. An avalanche had blocked the main highway out of town. Multiple vehicles had been caught unaware. Rescue teams were being deployed that moment.

"I can't believe this! Violet, don't your snow rangers watch for these kind of things?"

"You know we do." The conditions were ripe for avalanches, but not in that part of the forest and not the mountain next to that stretch of highway. The slope wasn't deep enough to make it a high-risk area, unless the avalanche had some help. "The explosives," she said simply.

The sheriff was answering his radio and either didn't hear her or decided not to acknowledge her. "I can't even get you to the station. We're going to have to turn around. Need to get this semi's attention and help him turn around first. Whoa. He's taking the curve way too fast." The sheriff managed to flip his lights on once before the truck's back trailer slid across the highway, folding like a jackknife.

Violet flung her arms up to protect her face as the sheriff slammed on his brakes. A second truck smashed into the back of the SUV. Her forearms struck the metal divider, and she bounced off the plastic seat. The screech of metal overloaded her senses as the vehicle slid off the road. The SUV didn't stop until the hood crashed into an evergreen tree. The sheriff's head hung at an unnatural angle, blood dripping from his forehead.

Hot pain vibrated through her bones as she fought to sit upright. The side passenger door opened and a man in a ski mask came into view. His eyes crinkled. "Let's try this again, shall we? Someone wants to have a chat with you."

He reached for her, and she kicked out her leg. The man grabbed her foot and twisted her leg around until her knee felt like it was going to dislocate. The opposite door opened, and another man grabbed her wrists with one hand. A needle hit her shoulder, and she lost the ability to fight.

FOURTEEN

Alex almost forgot to turn off Violet's pass-code option before the phone timed out. His fingers shook as he forwarded Daniella's information to his own phone. Teddy whined again. "I feel the same way, buddy. We're going to get her back before the day is done."

There he went again. Making promises about justice without being able to guarantee he could make them happen. He pulled the photograph from his pocket and realized he still had the photo of him and Rick, the one that Teddy had used to find the bomb. He needed to get this properly logged as evidence. Unfortunately, he didn't have any evidence bags, so he gingerly put that picture back in his pocket and zipped it closed.

Once he'd captured the photo of Bridget and Violet, he texted it to Daniella, careful to word the question without leading the witness. "Who do you see in this photo?" He signed it with his FBI agent logo he kept for official correspondence.

A quick call to Violet's lawyer, and then he would be on his way to the station. He didn't know if Daniella even had her cell phone in the hospital with—

His cell phone vibrated instantaneously.

Violet was so adorbs in college! The reporter has had some good plastic surgery, and this is no wig. If I had to guess, she's had a lift and some nose work, maybe a little cheek restructuring, but her eyes are the same. Totally her.

A second later, another text followed.

Did I break the case wide open?

He laughed aloud, despite the deputy's strange expression as he still cataloged evidence. No wonder Violet loved Daniella.

Actually, you did. Maybe you should consider criminal justice as a major.

He didn't wait for a response as he ran to Violet's vehicle. Teddy didn't need prompting to jump into his section in the back. "Let's go get her, boy."

They drove the winding, tree-lined road out of town but had only gotten to the town's outskirts when a pileup of traffic impeded their progress. Something wasn't right. Helicopters flew overhead. They headed in the same direction as the sheriff had taken Violet.

Someone wearing orange at the end of the line was organizing traffic. Vehicles began turning around and driving back the direction they'd all come from. This highway was the only way to go east out of town. Travelers would lose two hours going west to take the long way around, but that wouldn't lead him and Teddy back to the police station. Alex pulled over and let Teddy out of the vehicle.

They walked forward until they reached the first vehicle with windows down. "Do you know what's going on?"

"Avalanche ahead. To make matters worse, some semi jackknifed, taking down a police car with it."

Alex's ears roared and he didn't hear anything else. He jogged forward. Teddy slid to his right, his paws gliding over the snow as Alex's feet hit the wet pavement. Despite his arduous training regimen, Alex found himself out of breath as he pressed forward at a faster speed than he'd ever tried. Violet...

They rounded the curve of the highway, and flashing lights rallied him to put forth an extra burst of speed. Two officers saw him approaching and turned, waving their arms at him. He disregarded them, focusing only on the sight before him. The sheriff's SUV was smashed, crumpled into half its size, in between a pickup truck and a forty-foot tree.

He slid across the snow to a stop, searching for signs of Violet. An officer approached with his hands out. Alex shoved his badge in his direction. "I need to see Violet Sharp."

"Was she with the sheriff?"

Only then did he see a man on a stretcher being loaded into an ambulance. "Yes," he answered weakly.

The officer rattled off something about an escaped suspect. Never before had Alex wanted to punch a perfect stranger. "She's not." He shook his head. There was no time to waste trying to convince the officers. They could sort everything out after she was safe. "We're going to need backup. Get the K-9 officers from the forest service on the trail. Call the rangers and the troopers. She's been kidnapped. No time to explain. Make the calls."

"The resources are simply not available. The avalanche is the number-one priority. I'll make the calls, but until we've got all those people in their cars out of the snow, we've got to focus on the lives we can save now."

The officer turned around and seemed to be explaining to the other deputy what Alex had said. Teddy strained forward, sniffing. He reached the open door of the SUV and whined. When he looked over his shoulder at Alex, his sad golden eyes implored him. The dog wanted to work.

Would the Newfoundland even listen to him? Alex wasn't a trained handler, but this might be the only chance for Violet. "Find," he said tentatively.

Teddy's tail wagged so hard it hit the side of Alex's leg like a whip. He stepped to the side as the dog's head plunged into the snow. Instantly, his back and fluffy tail went rigid. Alex leaned over and unclipped the dog as he'd seen Violet do several times before. "Get her boy," he whispered. Teddy raced ahead, disappearing into the tree line.

"Call the rangers," he shouted over his shoulder. "Tell them we've found District Ranger Sharp's trail and need their help!"

He slid on his back down a small hill to keep up with Teddy. High knees through the snow were going to exhaust him fast. What he wouldn't do for a snowmobile now.

Thoughts of Violet being with Rick's killer kept his feet moving.

She'd forgiven him for being the one who had survived. That was what he'd thought he needed from her, and while his shoulders had felt the burden lift slightly, the uncomfortable sensation of shame had stubbornly remained. And now it felt like he was about to lose another partner. Her words about their time on snowmobiles returned to him. *Imagine if I'd told you to go left.*

He'd never expected her judgment to be perfect. His gut twisted with the double standard. Rick had certainly never held Alex to that high of a standard. He hadn't expected perfection from Rick, either. In fact, they'd called each other "my trusty old sidekick." As if the person who said it first was the real superhero.

For a joke, Alex had given Rick a six-inch trophy with a faceless man holding a sign that said World's Best Sidekick. From that moment on, they'd played a game where they tried to get that trophy into each other's possession. Using sleight of hand to do it had almost been like a training exercise. They'd each had ownership of the trophy numerous times. Though as far as Alex knew, Rick had the trophy last.

Alex certainly didn't feel like a superhero now. He never had been, though. Snow dropped from a branch overhead and fell on top of him like a wake-up call. He slipped and dropped to his knees. Teddy froze and looked over his shoulders, checking on him.

"Keep going." Alex struggled to his feet. His body might be worse for wear, but he felt a renewed purpose. He wasn't perfect, no. He was a desperate man. There would never be enough contingencies or perfect plans to avoid evil. He'd finally gotten that through his thick skull. He could only do his best and pray it would be enough.

He trudged forward after Teddy, almost on autopilot. All he desired was to keep Violet safe, but despite trying his best, he had no control over that.

Teddy's trajectory didn't waver. He knew the smell of his partner well. Alex understood more than ever why Violet hoped to help others gain the blessings of search-and-rescue dogs nearby. He wanted to help Violet make that dream come true. His words earlier hadn't been a slip of the tongue after all. He wanted *her* as his new partner, not for work but for life. Was the realization too little, too late?

Teddy stiffened and ducked his head in between two bushes. The snow was almost up to his belly. Alex waded until he was next to him and tried to see what had stolen Teddy's attention.

Roughly twenty feet away, two men sat on snowmobiles. One held binoculars and intently stared at something past the tree line. "As soon as she's done with the girl, it's all warm places from now on. Any minute now, we can join her and head for the helicopter. It's fueled and ready."

Done with the girl? His heart raced, and he put a hand on Teddy. "Shh," he whispered lest the dog decide to growl. He reached for his gun. The men also had weapons, and they were situated in such a way Alex couldn't aim at both of them at once. If he could distract them, he'd feel more confident about taking the pair on at the same time.

Teddy let out an exaggerated breath, complete with the smell of meat sticks. It was almost as if the dog was releasing a whispered bark. Tension radiated off Teddy, but he remained still as Alex kept a hand on top of his head.

"Looks like she's about to wake her up," one man said. "The fun's about to begin."

Alex's gut twisted with the implications. There was a space underneath the bushes without snow. Alex reached down and found a rock about the size of a grapefruit. It would do nicely. His gaze drifted upward to the thick branches full of snow above the snowmobiles. Enough to startle and disorient them if it fell on their heads, as he knew from experience. He lifted up a silent prayer that his pitching skills weren't as rusty as he feared.

"It's about time you woke up." The voice sounded familiar to Violet, but trying to lift her eyelids was a fight. The bright sunshine gave her an instant headache, and she squeezed her eyes closed again. Something about this situation was wrong, but her mind wasn't working fast enough to know what that was. Like reaching through a thick fog to get a coherent thought, she took stock of her senses.

Everything around her was cold and hard and smelled like clean air and pine. She went to move her hand to shield her eyes before trying to open them again, but her arm wouldn't budge. Her balance lost, she tipped over sideways into an ice-cold mound.

Unkind laughter broke through the murkiness of her mind. Her adrenaline spiked, and she jolted upright, now fully awake. A woman with long red hair in a white coat and snowsuit was crouched down, her nose almost touching Violet's. "I'm tired of waiting for you. All I've done is wait for you lately."

"Bridget."

The woman grinned and straightened. She brushed a hand down her hair. "Like my new look?"

"Your new face?" Violet struggled to

move into a better position, except her hands were tied behind her back. Her teeth began chattering, and her muscles tightened, trying to get warm.

"Would you have recognized me without our little chat?"

"No." Violet said, staring at her own shoes until they came into focus. She flicked a gaze at the woman. The voice was the same, and the eyes. Bridget had a pout on her face, meaning she wanted Violet to recognize her. Fine. She'd play along. "You're still just as self-centered, though. Would it be better if I called you the Firecracker?"

Bridget clapped. "You *do* remember. See? I knew Rick would, too. That's why he had to go first." She made tsk-tsk sounds. "I blame his obsession with crossword puzzles. Kept his memory too sharp. I knew he'd never forget our time together."

Violet fought against waves of nausea by breathing through her nose. There was no getting out of this alive, but she wanted to die fighting. Maybe she could stop Bridget from taking more innocent lives. She needed time to wake up more, to get the knots untied, but that meant encouraging Bridget's ego to be on display and to talk about Rick's death. "You became the Firecracker's copycat."

Bridget's nostrils flared, and she pursed her lips. "No. I took over for him. Found him on an abandoned ranch before the feds did. They had no idea how close they came, but they gave up too soon. I eventually found where he was hiding on the ranch. I like to think his hairbrush was a gift to me so his legacy could live on—"

"Legacy? Your way of concealing your identity, you mean?" The first knot around her wrists gave way.

"They'll never know the Firecracker had an unfortunate accident when I came to visit him. Like the one you're going to have." Bridget stepped aside.

A set of USFS explosives sat wired together in such a way that they would create a bigger blast than was needed for an avalanche. There had to be at least twice as many explosives here as there'd been underneath the SUV at the resort. Violet forced her expression to remain neutral. Bridget always did thrive on drama, and Violet needed more time. "And when Rick was almost on to you, you killed him."

"It's amazing what a good informant can lead the FBI to do."

In that moment, Violet knew that Rick's death hadn't been an attempted assignation. It'd all been theater, which meant Alex's arrival here must've been orchestrated by Bridget, as well. "You planted tips with the informants. You never intended to carry out an assassination here."

"That's where you're wrong. Rick was a strategic play. I had hoped to kill Alex first. I wanted Rick to figure out it was me before I killed him." She shrugged. "But Rick was faster to the bomb than

Alex, so we never had a moment like this. Believe it or not, I had considered simply ruining your life and letting you live. Guess I've gotten more sentimental than I like to think." Her lip curled. "Oh, don't worry. I'll take care of Mark Leonard before he becomes the federal nominee. Just like I got the delegate Rick was trying to keep me from. It actually helps my reputation if there's one or two who get away. They increase their security, and then I still get them anyway."

She couldn't handle the glee in the woman's voice any longer. "What exactly do you want from me?"

Bridget's face transformed into a sneer. "For you to see that *you* made me the Firecracker. You only have yourself to blame for Rick's death. You'd be nothing without me, but you betrayed me more than anyone. You took away Rick, my friends and my career." She shrugged. "I still thrived, but you needed to feel what it's like when everyone turns against you.

And now you know exactly who made that happen. Everyone in your life will remember you as a criminal."

"I've been drugged, so maybe I'm a little slow, but how do you figure? You're the one who tried to ruin my life in college. You're the one who tried to get me expelled." The moment she said the words, she realized it'd do no good. Now she understood what Alex had meant about having to at least try.

"I only tried to help you, Violet. Look at you. I knew, before you ever did, that you were never cut out for criminal justice. Managing forest employees? What a waste of your training, the training *I* could have had. If you hadn't turned on me, maybe you would've spared yourself some pain, huh? Rick would still be alive, happy with me."

Violet ignored the bait. The second knot slipped open. One knot to go. If only her fingers would stop stinging from the cold. She was starting to lose feeling in her pinkie, and pain radiated up her forearms. "Fine. Why'd you take Rick's stuff?"

"I couldn't risk that he'd kept any of our correspondence. I needed to make sure nothing would lead to me after you were gone."

"Hate to break it to you, but he didn't keep a thing."

"You probably burned them. That would be so like you."

Violet forced herself to not roll her eyes. "You don't have to do this, Bridget. You could stop hurting people. Go and live a different life, helping others even."

Bridget flashed a smug grin. "And leave you as a witness?"

"We both know you excel at pretending to be dead. People see what they want to see." As she said the words, she realized that's what she'd been doing the past couple of years. She'd viewed her friends as doing just fine, not having their own problems. And she'd decided to believe she could never experience love and happiness again. She quietly lifted a prayer of thanks that her eyes had been opened.

Bridget had been seeing what she chose to see for years, and her twisted reality had allowed her to justify murder. "As if I would believe Miss Perfect Violet wants me to get away with my crimes." Bridget shook her head. "Nice try."

"Of course that's not what I want!" Violet's voice rose, her jaw tight with tension. Her entire being shook, and she struggled to locate the last knot. "I want justice for my husband." Her eyes stung, and her neck felt strangled as she struggled to keep back a sob. "The countless lives he would've affected had he still been alive," she whispered. "But since when did you care what I want?" She finally made herself lift her gaze to look at Bridget again. "You could still stop."

The woman stared at her, and for a second, the Bridget she knew made an appearance. Until a gust of wind blew her red hair back into the breeze. Bridget tilted her head and picked up a rifle off the snowmobile next to her. She approached Violet again and bent over until their faces were mere inches apart. "What people like you will never understand is there will always be those who do the controlling and those who are controlled. I'll never be the pawn again."

Those weren't the only two categories of people, but now that Bridget held the rifle in her hand, Violet had regained her self-control and remained silent.

Bridget straightened. "Besides, I did you a favor. Rick was holding you back. With him gone, you finally realized where you belonged." She smiled. "In a backwoods hole. Like I said, you should never have gone into law enforcement." She exaggerated a fake pout. "Can't say I didn't warn you. Though I have to give you credit, you put up a tougher fight than my men expected. But that only made it more fun for me."

A bark carried over the hushed landscape. Violet stiffened. She knew that bark, but she refused to look. Bridget straightened and swung around. Violet followed the woman's gaze into the trees to the east. Nothing.

A snowmobile engine in the distance revved.

"That's my cue. My helicopter ride will be waiting for me."

Through the tree line, flashes of a snowmobile appeared. It looked like Alex was driving with Teddy seated behind him, paws on his shoulders. They were coming for her, but they'd be in danger if they got any closer. So far, Bridget hadn't noticed them, and Violet couldn't let her.

Bridget pulled out a small device that Violet recognized as the remote timer to the explosives. She clicked the device and winked at Violet.

Violet finally felt the last knot give and moved to pull her hands apart, but her wrists wouldn't budge. One knot still held. She'd miscounted. Violet buried her face into her bent knees. The only time she'd ever felt this helpless was when she'd found out Rick was dead, and now Teddy and Alex might die with her.

"Ah, that's the kind of goodbye I was hoping to see." Bridget squatted down in front of her and sneered. "You should have never crossed me, Violet."

The woman stood up, clearly pleased with herself. Bridget loved getting the last word, and Violet couldn't let her. She needed more time.

"The thing is, your men were fighting me when I still believed I had nothing to fight for." Violet stared her down, and Bridget's eyes widened ever so slightly, curious. "Imagine how I would fight if I thought I did." Violet slid on her back and kicked her legs against Bridget's heels in one smooth motion.

Bridget's boots flew out from under her. She landed on her back, and the remote flew up in the air and landed ten feet off, disappearing in a snow pile. The rifle slid a few inches away, but Bridget pounced on it before Violet had so much as a chance.

"I've got company. Where are you?" Bridget snapped into a radio.

Static filled the air as a male voice Violet adored answered, "Change of plans. They're tied up."

Despite the pain, Violet couldn't help but smile as she struggled to flip over and get up without the use of her hands. Two figures broke into the open, their snowmobile bouncing over the mountainous slope.

The click of a rifle chilled her bones. "Let's give them a little welcome gift, shall we?"

Though her vision was blurry, she knew in an instant that Teddy and Alex were rushing toward their deaths.

FIFTEEN

Violet didn't wait for Bridget to fire. She slammed into Bridget's torso, and a bullet soared into the air.

Bridget screamed and jabbed Violet underneath the ribs with the butt of the rifle, forcing all air out of her lungs. She hunched over, opening her mouth, with no oxygen to relieve her pain. Five seconds later, her lungs greedily pulled in air. She panted and righted herself just in time to see Bridget hop on a snowmobile and shoot down the fastest route of the mountains, away from the set of explosives at Violet's feet.

Violet took off running, narrowly avoiding falling on her face with each step. Never before had she missed the use of her arms and hands this much. She screamed, "Go away! Go back!" Her voice was weak, and she shook her head as dramatically as she could. They couldn't die saving her.

Fifty feet away, Alex's snowmobile sank into the mounds, and the engine sputtered. He'd choked it. Teddy jumped off the back without waiting for Alex, bounding through the drifts as if to prepare for a happy reunion. "No! Run away!"

Alex did his best to keep up with Teddy until he reached her. Teddy kept running for something and wasn't listening to her for the first time in years. Alex stepped around her and grabbed her wrists.

He wasn't listening to her either. "You have to go. Now."

"Only with you. You'll be much better at driving us out of here on the snowmobile than I will be."

"You don't understand. The explosives! They're on a timer. I don't know how long we have, but it will be any second. She's made her getaway." The ropes mercifully dropped from her wrists and she spun around to face him.

He lifted his face. "Where'd she put the bombs?"

A gunshot rang out. Blood splattered the white terrain around them. Alex's eyes grew wide as he fell to the ground. She felt like her body was moving slower than her mind demanded as she turned to see Bridget perched on her snowmobile with her rifle in hand. The woman returned to her seat and sped off again.

Violet dropped to her knees. "Alex..." She swallowed back a sob. There was no time to fall apart. "Look at me. Where were you shot?" His coat looked intact, but she couldn't tell where the bullet might have penetrated his black jeans. Her focus kept sliding to the blood on the ground.

"I... I'm not sure."

"We have to get you out of here!"

Alex paled, but his eyes weren't on her face. She followed his gaze to see Teddy had picked up the set of explosives in his mouth and had bounded in the opposite direction. She didn't remember screaming, but she heard her dog's name echo off the mountain walls. All she could think about was the other Newfoundland who had tried to get an explosive far from the people he loved. That dog had died a hero. "He can't die!" she cried. She fought to get up, but if she went after her dog, would that mean Alex would die?

Another bullet sped through the air, throwing up snow mere feet from Teddy. Would this woman never give up? The dog didn't so much as flinch. He continued sprinting due west with the package. "Take my weapon." Alex moaned, as if the words took extra effort. She grabbed his gun, stood and sighted down the mountain at where Bridget had once again stopped.

Violet shot off a few bullets, but her aim was shoddy, given the way her fingers fought to grip the gun. The shots were close enough to encourage Bridget to take off on her snowmobile again. Soon, the woman would be too far away for her rifle to do any harm.

"Teddy," she called again, losing hope. "There's a sudden drop-off to the west. He's getting too close." Maybe she could try to find the drift the remote had fallen into, but there had to be at least a dozen, and she couldn't remember which one it was. She moved to dive into the closest one to search. Fingers wrapped around her wrist. Alex had gotten back up.

"Violet, he's trying to save you. Let him do his job." Alex's fingers lost their grip as he stumbled backward, falling into the snow.

He was right, though it was hard to think straight or see through her tears. Her partner's lifesaving instinct would not be deterred, so she had to do her part. She reached for Alex. "Have you figured out where you were hit?"

"Not sure. Upper thigh, I think."

Blood pooled in the snow at an alarming rate. If the bullet had hit an artery, it was game over. Even if it hadn't, blood loss was a serious risk. She leaned over and helped Alex to stand again. "Drape your weight over me. As much as you can. Try to apply pressure to the wound with your other arm."

In the worst three-legged race ever, they rushed back to the snowmobile. Her ribs felt like they were being stretched apart as she maneuvered the vehicle out of the deep pit it had sunken into. "Teddy," she called out again, her voice breaking. "Teddy, please come!"

"He is," Alex said into her ear over the hum of the machine. "He is coming!"

She squinted through the blowing snow. Her beautiful brown dog's fur was flying in the wind. His tongue hung out to the side as he tore through the drifts with the same tenacity as he swam through alpine lakes. He was almost to them! They might just make it—

The earth shook. Alex wrapped his arm around her waist. "Drive!" Sheets of white at the far west edge, just past the drop-off, peeled off the slope and magnified into a giant white plume heading straight for Teddy...and them.

Alex reached around Violet for the handlebars. A cry tore from her throat as they twisted the snowmobile's steering together in a hard left. Even though his chest hadn't been hit, the searing pain at the thought of Teddy caught in the avalanche felt like it would kill him. He had to make the dog's sacrifice worth it and help save Violet.

He kept his head hitched over Violet's shoulder to see, but it was pointless. Tears had blurred his vision. Half a second later, the snow wiped out visibility. Like a hand had grabbed the back of the vehicle and shoved them forward, they flew off the machine. Gravity's cruel game slammed him down, provoking his scream when his gunshot wound was smacked hard. He lost sight of Violet, and snow pelted him for a good twenty seconds before he regained his other senses.

And then there was silence, somehow louder than any of the sounds before. About an inch or two of icy powder coated his face and chest, but he wasn't buried. Teddy had taken the bomb over a cliff of sorts and diverted the avalanche far enough away that they'd survived the explosion. He flipped over on his hands and knees and searched the sea of white. Violet sat up, brushing her hands over her face. She was alive! Her eyes met his, anguish written all over her face.

He diverted his gaze to a hundred yards or so past her to where he guessed Teddy had been. There could still be a chance. Violet followed his gaze and jumped up. "Teddy!"

Alex fought off the waves of dizziness and joined her. His backside was going numb, whether that was a good sign or not, he wasn't sure. For now, he had to help save Teddy.

They stumbled in the deep drifts, falling and righting themselves over and over. "The snow sets like concrete in two minutes after an avalanche. If you're underneath, you have no idea which way is up or down, and which way to dig, but Teddy still has his nose. He should be able to smell, and maybe he'll hear us."

They began hollering for the dog nonstop, crawling over the mounds that were becoming a hard fortress under their hands and knees. Snow sputtered ten feet from Alex's face, smacking the top of his head. A brown paw appeared, followed by the golden eyes he'd come to love.

"Teddy!" Violet began laughing and crying and crawled toward him. The dog bounded into her arms, and she landed on her back with the dog's paws on top of her shoulders.

The sheets of white had settled all the way down the mountain, and far below, he spotted another snowmobile. Only its nose was visible, sticking into the air. Teddy had ensured the avalanche would hit Bridget's escape route. Alex's leg lost all strength, and he dropped into the snow, looking up at the crystal-clear blue sky. If he was going to die, at least his heart was at peace. He just had one more thing he'd like to do.

"Alexander Driscoll, don't you dare die on me!"

He couldn't help but laugh at the use of his full name. "I'm trying my best, Violet, but I need to tell you something."

"Teddy, get him warm." She ran past him to the snowmobile. "Pray the radio still works on this thing."

He only half heard her as the dog lay down beside him, his heavy head on his chest. The static of radio could be heard as Violet sent out an SOS. A moment later, a voice came through.

"This is Ranger Alatorres. Anyone on this line?"

"Yes! This is District Ranger Sharp. Assistance needed. Special Agent Driscoll has been shot. Medic needed."

"Tell them we need an avalanche dog for Bridget." His leg was regaining feeling again, and he groaned, not realizing what a blessing numbness had been before. Teddy shifted off him and rested at his side. He didn't hear the rest of Violet's hastily worded orders to the rangers, but a second later, her face was above his. "Help is on the way. A helicopter for you, and a German shepherd and handcuffs for Bridget, if she's alive down there."

His breath had grown hot and shallow, but all that mattered was he was with Violet. "I'm scared you won't want to see me again after I tell you this, but I—"

"I love you." She reached for both sides of his face.

He frowned, a little confused but relishing her touch, even if her fingers were freezing cold. "It was that obvious what I was going to say, huh?" Although he was hoping to say it out loud, he was secretly pleased she already understood. "Please know that I would never ever try to replace Rick or diminish his memory. I understand if it's too painful, but I had to tell you."

"What are you talking about?" She blinked rapidly. "I'm trying to say *I* love *you*, Alex." Her breath came out in a staccato rhythm, as if she couldn't get a full breath. "I don't know what the future might hold, but I love you." A tear slid down her cheek.

"You do?" His heart jumped to his throat. "But *I* love *you*."

She laughed. "Well, you don't have to sound annoyed."

"Not annoyed. Shocked." He grinned. "And incredibly grateful." His fingers shook as he slid his hands behind her neck. His eyes searched hers, looking for permission. Instead of giving it, she leaned forward and pressed her lips against his. His heart surged, and a wave of dizziness washed over him, though that was likely from the bullet wound. He hoped for another chance to prove his theory.

Approaching snowmobiles and whirring chopper blades above interrupted the moment. Violet sat up, and Alex held her hand while wrapping his other arm around Teddy. So this was what it was like to want a family. "Violet, before I pass out, I need to ask you a question."

Her mouth dropped open. "What is it?"

"Do you and Teddy have any plans for New Year's Eve?"

Her entire face lit up. "What'd you have in mind?" She gave him a side-eye. "More undercover work?"

"I was thinking more along the lines of a real first date." He patted Teddy. "As long as your partner approves."

Teddy kissed the side of his face, and Violet tilted her head back and laughed.

"No kisses! From now on, I'm the only who does the honors." And she leaned over and did just that.

EPILOGUE

Six months later

Violet pulled into the small parking lot of the Military Reserve in Boise. The rustic park was equidistant between her work at the Boise National Forest and the FBI satellite office at the courthouse.

The June air was pleasant, not too cold or hot for a late afternoon. She and Teddy followed Alex's directions up a scenic trail to a spot overlooking the Treasure Valley. Next to a field of wildflowers, Alex was placing a picnic basket on top of a quilt. He spotted them and rushed over. He patted Teddy on the head while pulling her into a hug.

This was her chance. Over the past

few months, she'd discovered notes and trinkets in her coat pockets during work hours. Alex used his sleight-of-hand training to leave her surprises to find later at work, and she had been wanting to return the favor. Except, thus far, he'd caught her every time she made a move for his pockets. Today, he didn't seem to notice. She'd finally done it.

He pulled back and did a double take at her smile. "What? You have a twinkle in your eye."

She shrugged. "It's been a good day. In fact, I took an unplanned day off."

He registered his surprise. "Any reason?"

"I received a shipment first thing this morning. Rick's stuff is no longer considered evidence." Bridget had been convicted on so many charges she would never be getting out. Especially since Violet had passed on the news about her finding the real Firecracker at a ranch.

They'd reevaluated their DNA leads and taken a cadaver dog with them to the property.

"I wondered when that would happen." He slid his hands to the top of her shoulders, and his eyes narrowed in concern. "How are you doing?"

"I'm okay, really. I'm thankful to have them back." She breathed a sigh of relief at the confirmation that she really meant it. She'd spent hours poring over the photos and notes, and while her heart still squeezed with the memories and the pain of loss, the grief had changed. She no longer felt broken into a million pieces whenever she thought of Rick. Instead, she felt just a little bit closer to him.

Alex watched her closely. "I'm glad. I hope to look at them someday, too. When you're ready." His own smile magnified.

"Funny you should mention that. I can finally give something to you that I'm sure he'd want you to have. Except, I think you already have it."

He raised an eyebrow and pursed his lips. His eyes widened as he patted down his pockets. "You got me, didn't you?"

"I think Rick would've wanted it that way."

Alex pulled out a small golden trophy from his jacket that read World's Greatest Sidekick. He tipped his head back, and a delicious laugh filled the air. She'd known he'd love it.

A bittersweet smile crossed Alex's face. She understood. Rick would always be missed. Alex lifted his eyes to hers. "I'm impressed." He held up the sidekick trophy. "Though, I know now not to deny this title. There's only one true superhero in our midst."

He gave a knowing glance at Teddy, who wagged his tail in response.

"Agreed."

Alex set down the trophy, unlatched

the picnic basket and pulled out a gift bag. "First, a little something for you and Teddy."

She opened the bag to find several framed photographs of Teddy. "They're beautiful."

"I thought he deserved to have his own inspiration wall for other dogs to take a look at." He shrugged. "That is if you still want that property off State Street. The owner has agreed to let you put in an offer before it goes to market."

She gasped and set down the frames to pull Alex into a tight embrace. "Yes!" She'd been working many nights and weekends on her business plan for the search-and-rescue school. She'd been dreaming about that location, which was propped right in between the city and the trails leading into the foothills. "Should I call him now?"

He laughed. "Tomorrow should be soon enough." Alex pulled out a treat from his inside jacket pocket. "And, speaking of Teddy—" he unwrapped it and offered it to the dog "—would you mind if I have a moment alone with your partner? I have something of a sensitive nature to discuss with her."

Teddy flopped down on the quilt and tilted the meat stick with his paws so he could properly enjoy it.

Alex turned back and took her hand. "I'm trying to remain calm, but I have to admit, I'm really hoping you succeeded with a one-handed switch when you put the statue in my pocket."

The little box she'd switched out felt hot in her own pocket. The one time she'd actually managed to pull a sleight of hand seemed very dangerous now. Her cheeks felt on fire, and her heart pounded in her chest. "I didn't look at it. I didn't have an opportunity. It's in my pocket. You want it back now?"

He dropped to his knee. "Would you be willing to open it instead?"

Her breath caught, but she didn't dare hope. It could be something innocuous like a necklace or a pair of earrings.

"This is one of those times you probably already know what I'm going to ask," he said softly.

She pulled out the box, and the black velvet beckoned her. Alex placed a hand on top of the case and flipped it open. The setting sun hit the diamond ring, and beams erupted from the dazzling prisms.

"I know you have a partner in your work, but I'd like to ask you to be my partner in life. I love you, Violet."

She bit her bottom lip, willing her tongue to remain silent until he finished.

He grinned. "You're biting your lip again. I think I finally understand what that means."

"Don't you have a question to ask?"

He laughed. "Violet, will you please do me the honor of being—"

"Yes, I'll be your wife!" The words burst

from her mouth, followed by a laugh. "I'm sorry."

"I'm not." He jumped up and turned to Teddy. "She said yes!"

Teddy lifted his head, and if ever a dog could smile, hers did. Right before he returned to his treat, at least. Her vision grew blurry as Alex closed the distance between them. He gently touched her cheeks, his thumbs wiping away the few tears that had escaped. He gently kissed the sides of her face. "I love you," he whispered.

"I love you, too."

He pulled back for the briefest of moments to look at her, his own eyes glistening. Then he kissed her soundly, wrapping his arm around her waist and pulling her closer. A paw landed on top of her shoulder, and they broke apart, laughing at Teddy's attempt to give kisses of his own. Violet wondered at the wisdom of teaching Teddy to stand on his hind legs. She also marveled at the last six months. She and Alex were done hiding from life and love, and their own personal superhero would make sure they kept it that way.

* * * * *

K-9 Search and Rescue
Search and Defend *by*
Heather Woodhaven
Following the Trail *by Lynette Eason*
Dangerous Mountain Rescue *by*
Christy Barritt

Dear Reader,

I hope you enjoyed Alex and Violet's journey to each other. If I looked back at all the letters at the end of my books, I'd probably find a proclamation that each book was the hardest to write. This one would be no different. Writing Teddy, however, was the easiest character I've ever written. The inspiration wall filled with framed photos of other Newfoundland dogs was also my personal writing inspiration at my desk. I respect the difficulty of training such a dog, and I marvel at their lifesaving abilities.

As always, I enjoy hearing from readers and send out occasional updates on new releases in my newsletter. You can reach me at HeatherWoodhaven.com.

I hope your new year is filled with hopes, dreams and new adventures.

Sincerely,
Heather Woodhaven